FLIRTING WITH SUNSHINE

by

J. Sterling

Thank you for purchasing this book.

I hope you enjoy my Fun for the Holidays collection!

Sign up for my newsletter to get emails about new releases, upcoming releases, and special price promotions:

NEWSLETTER

Come join my private reader group on Facebook for giveaways:

PRIVATE READER GROUP

facebook.com/groups/ThePerfectGameChangerGroup

Other Books by J. Sterling

Bitter Rivals—an enemies to lovers romance

Dear Heart, I Hate You

10 Years Later—A Second Chance Romance

In Dreams—a new adult college romance

Chance Encounters—a coming-of-age story

THE GAME SERIES

The Perfect Game—Book One

The Game Changer—Book Two

The Sweetest Game—Book Three

The Other Game (Dean Carter)—Book Four

THE PLAYBOY SERIAL

Avoiding the Playboy—Episode #1

Resisting the Playboy—Episode #2

Wanting the Playboy—Episode #3

THE CELEBRITY SERIES

Seeing Stars—Madison & Walker

Breaking Stars—Paige & Tatum

Losing Stars—Quinn & Ryson

THE FISHER BROTHERS SERIES

No Bad Days—a New Adult, Second Chance Romance
Guy Hater—an Emotional Love story
Adios Pantalones—a Single Mom Romance
Happy Ending

THE BOYS OF BASEBALL
(THE NEXT GENERATION OF FULLTON STATE BASEBALL
PLAYERS)
The Ninth Inning—Cole Anders
Behind the Plate—Chance Carter
Safe at First—Mac Davies

FUN FOR THE HOLIDAYS
(A COLLECTION OF STAND-ALONE NOVELS WITH HOLIDAY-
BASED THEMES)
Kissing my Co-worker
Dumped for Valentine's
My Week with the Prince
Fools in Love
Spring's Second Chance
Don't Marry Him
Summer Lovin'
Flirting with Sunshine
Falling for the Boss
Tricked by my Ex
The Thanksgiving Hookup
Christmas with Saint

GOOD MORNING
AVA

T HE SUN WAS just starting to rise, and I was already on my second cup of coffee. I'd always woken up early, even before the restaurant was my sole responsibility. As a child, I'd adored my father so much that I emulated whatever he did, just to be around him more. That included waking up before most people even thought about hitting the snooze button for the first time. He'd been gone for almost a year now, and I still missed him at every sunrise.

Meow. My cat, Snickers, wrapped her soft body around my feet, begging for attention.

Reaching down, I picked her up with both arms and patted her on the head. She purred loud—a sure sign that she enjoyed that scratch behind the ears.

"You like that?" I asked, and she continued making the

vibrating noise, her head pushing against my palm in a silent demand for more.

Snickers had been a haggard-looking stray at first, hanging around the restaurant, begging for scraps. I started leaving her a little dish of food, an array of whatever was leftover at the end of the night, but she never let me get anywhere near her. One step in her direction, and she bolted like I was going to snatch her up and put her on the menu.

It took six long months before she trusted me enough to let me touch her tail. *Just* her tail.

And then, one night, after I'd had a particularly long day filled with drunk tourists, she followed me up the stairs outside the restaurant and walked right into my apartment like she owned the place. I'd watched her meander from room to room before hopping up onto the couch and settling on top of a pillow, claiming it.

From that moment on, I became the proud owner of the fattest tabby cat you'd ever seen in your life.

A group of silhouettes moving like a choreographed dance caught my eye, and I put Snickers down, so I could focus. Holding her for too long was a workout most arms couldn't take. Mine were used to it by now. What I felt like I'd never get used to was seeing Tony Garcia, all tanned skin and flexing muscles from his job on the water, with his multicolored dog following his every move.

Tony had shown up in our sleepy town like a breath of fresh air, breezing in without warning and settling down in a house not far from my own. I assumed he liked being close to his boat, the same way I enjoyed living above my restaurant. It was comforting to know that if anything went wrong, I was only a few steps away from being able to solve it—or at least attempting to. You see, when you worked for yourself, certain things just hit a little differently, like location and timing and the fact that I was a bit of a freak who didn't like to give up any control to others.

He was a fisherman, new to our waters, and I bought fresh fish from him multiple days a week, depending on what I needed and what season we were in. My attraction to him had sprung to life when he sold me his morning catch that very first time. It had caught me off guard, throwing me for an unexpected loop, but I didn't think he'd even so much as cracked a smile in my direction in nine months. The guy couldn't be less interested in me or any other female in town, it seemed, so I refused to take it personally. Well, I tried not to. It was hard though.

Tony was like Snickers, I'd decided. He simply needed some wearing down.

Hmm ... maybe if I left a bowl of food for him outside my front door each night, he'd eventually come inside.

As I laughed to myself, my voice caught in my throat, and I coughed, pounding on my chest. Tony was looking up in my direction, clearly able to see me through my kitchen windows. He gave a slight wave with his hand before turning around and getting back to work, reminding me that I needed to do the same.

It had always been the plan for me to run the family restaurant when the time was right. And even though my ex-husband, Liam, had known that fact, he still tried to take me away from here permanently. While he went off to college after high school, I stayed back home and learned the ropes from my dad, knowing that, one day, it would all be mine. Or more accurately ... all *ours*.

Once Liam graduated, he got offered an entry-level position at the financial company he'd interned at for the past two years. He proposed to me and filled my hopeful, young head with all kinds of promises. The kind that you were willing to bet on because you were so in love that you convinced yourself that nothing could ever go wrong.

My moving to the big city was supposed to only be temporary—a handful of years at the most. Liam would make a name for himself in the firm before opening a remote office back here in Port Rufton, taking on new clients the company hadn't considered or reached before, while I ran the restaurant with my dad before taking it over completely.

I naively believed the narrative Liam had sold me in the beginning. Or maybe he had truly meant it at the time. I couldn't be sure, but something seemed to change along the way. Too many years started passing by with no mention of relocating or my running the restaurant. Liam kept getting promoted, and the allure of something bigger and better was always waiting around the next corner. He just needed to work longer hours in order to reach it, and then our future would be "all set."

I finally put it together that Liam never planned on bringing us back home, no matter what he said to the contrary. It was all lies to buy himself more time. He assumed that once too much time had passed, I'd give up on my dreams and do nothing but support his.

We started fighting … *viciously*.

He started cheating … *voraciously*.

I eventually found the strength to leave.

And, yes, I took half of what he had acquired. And, no, I didn't feel bad about it.

My dad got sick soon after and was too weak to keep going. I was grateful that I'd been back home for a few months by then, working side by side with him, learning everything I truly needed to keep the business running smoothly and successfully. I wouldn't have thought that much had changed over the years while I was away, but I was wrong. Time was always moving forward, and keeping up with it was a must. I'd been impressed when I learned my dad had hired a local teenager to run his social media accounts.

Losing him had been like a blow to the guts; it'd hurt, it'd ached, and it'd stolen my breath without warning.

I was grateful that I saw my mom almost every day. She stopped by the restaurant to drop off her homemade desserts—things you wouldn't typically think paired well with a seafood meal, but still got purchased nonetheless.

The one thing I could count on was that my mother's creations would sell out daily. Port Rufton loved Rosalinda's sweets. I'd been trying to convince her to open a bakery for as long as I could remember, but she wasn't the least bit interested. I thought one food business in the family was enough for her.

A hard knock on my door almost made me drop my coffee mug. Padding over, I pulled it open and tried to play it cool. Tony was on the other side, his smoldering glare staring at me like my existence bothered him somehow, his adorable dog sitting like a good boy at his feet.

"Fish is ready," he said with a nod toward the wharf.

"I'll be right down." I gave him my signature grin, but he turned away, unfazed. "Good morning, Tony. It's nice to see you. You look good today. Did you have fun on the water? Of course you did."

I continued shouting out ridiculous things, but he only huffed. Or maybe it was a grunt. I couldn't really tell, but no words followed any of his annoyed sounds. This was part of my morning routine; one of the fishermen would let me know they were ready, and then I would walk down and hand-select the pieces I'd use that day. The guys always gave me first access to their catch. I wasn't really sure why, but I appreciated it all the same.

I always bought my seafood fresh, local from the ocean right outside the window, and rarely stocked for more than one day at a time. If there were any leftovers after we closed for the night, they would get incorporated into a dish the very next day. Just like any fresh food or produce, fish was better when it was cooked quickly. Plus, the last thing I needed was someone getting sick and claiming it was my restaurant that had done it to them.

Social media these days could be brutal if someone posted the wrong thing regardless of how accurate it was or not. People usually didn't take the time to seek out the facts anymore. They simply bought into whatever they read, depending on who had said it. So, in all fairness, the opposite was also true. And those complimentary posts had brought in tons of new people to my restaurant over the last year and a half. I knew because they had told me.

We saw it online. So and so posted how much she loved the desserts here. I read this is the best place for lobster rolls and fish cakes.

I walked over to my couch and reached for my shoes before sitting down and pulling them on. Snickers hopped up next to me, pushing her head into my arm as I tried to work at tying them.

"Okay, okay," I said, giving her some extra love before standing tall with a grin. "How do I look?" I asked, and she meowed her approval. "Thanks. I'll be right back."

Snickers meowed again, and I pretended like I knew exactly what she was saying.

"Of course I'll bring you a treat."

As I headed toward the front door, Snickers moved from the couch and hopped up onto the kitchen counter, taking her place at the window, where she could watch me the whole time, her tail wagging like she was up to something devious. I wondered what she did when I wasn't around. Rolling my eyes, I silently cursed at myself for the crazy cat woman I'd suddenly become. I really needed to get out more.

SOLITUDE & PUNISHMENT
TONY

I WASN'T IMMUNE to the charms of Ava Starling, which was why I did my best to limit my contact with the woman. She was stunning in an unexpected manner. And I only meant that she didn't go out of her way to make sure she was *presentable* whenever she was in public.

I couldn't count on both hands the number of times I'd seen her without a stitch of makeup on—it had been so many times. Not that she needed any—I wasn't saying that. It was refreshing, the way she naturally glowed and danced around in her kitchen, creating meals that the men out here drooled over … and constantly talked about. She was a talented chef, although she scoffed whenever anyone called her that.

And she was *always. So. Happy.*

Which was another reason why I stayed away from

her. Happiness was the last thing I deserved. Not after what I'd done. After everything I'd destroyed. I planned on punishing myself until the day I died, avoiding people who were the epitome of sunshine and goodness, like Ava, no matter how attracted I was to her or how jealous I got when the other guys talked about trying to get her into bed. My feelings toward her were irrational and illogical … and had to be ignored.

I would never deserve someone as sweet as her. Not ever again.

I spotted Ava walking down the pathway toward the group of us, a huge grin on her face, like usual, as she pulled two rolling coolers behind her frame, like she always did.

Fishing in other cities was highly regulated, and you had to go through middlemen in order to sell your catch once it was off your boat. There were unions and all sorts of people with their hands in our pockets, sharing in our profits without doing any of the actual hard work. Selling directly to restaurants and businesses was typically forbidden, but this town had established their own rules back in the 1800s, and it had never been overturned, no matter how many times someone had tried. As long as the population stayed under a certain number, we were allowed to continue selling directly without any real regulatory fees or overlords.

"Morning, Rory." Ava's voice echoed through the crisp morning air as she stopped at his table, doling out compliments and inspecting his latest haul.

She always came to my station last, and I knew she did it on purpose. It was her way of torturing me, of making me watch her flirt with and charm every man on this dock until it was my turn for a sliver of her attention. I'd never let her know how much she got to me though. *I couldn't.* If I let my guard down even once around her, I'd fall in two seconds flat, and that wasn't part of my new life plan here. A plan that basically consisted of two words—solitude and punishment.

When Ava walked away from Rory's table, he started wrapping up her purchases. He'd deliver them to her restaurant, just like he did every morning, never letting her carry them herself.

Kiss-ass.

I hated how much he wanted her, but she never seemed

to give him a second thought, treating him the same way she treated all of us fishermen.

Rory loved to throw it in my face that they had dated once in junior high school, but that was a hundred years ago, so who gave a shit about that? Not me. And clearly not Ava either, or they'd still be dating. At least, that was what I kept trying to tell myself.

Rory looked up, his eyes meeting mine before he opened his big, fat mouth.

"I'm gonna do it soon," he yelled, and I knew exactly what he was referring to.

"So you keep saying," I challenged, hating myself for pushing him to do the one thing I wouldn't be able to handle watching and wouldn't be able to avoid seeing.

"Just wait." He grinned, and I wanted to walk right over to his table and sock him in the jaw.

Like I'd said earlier, *irrational*.

"I don't give a shit," I grumbled, but apparently, it was loud enough for him to hear because he laughed.

"That's obvious," he responded sarcastically.

To be fair, Rory wasn't a bad guy. He was just the most vocal when it came to his feelings for Ava. The available guys in this town all had some sort of crush on her—or, that was what I'd been told pretty early on after I moved here.

"Get in line," and, "Take a number," were the two most common phrases tossed in my direction whenever I so much as glanced at her in public.

It made sense though, considering the fact that this place was the size of a freaking pea. Who else were you supposed to want to date? A tourist who was only here temporarily and had bigger aspirations than settling down in a place no one had ever heard of before? Coupling up seemed like a challenge. Which was why it was so perfect for me. I needed to be alone.

I had, however, found it a little odd how protective the people seemed to be over her until I heard bits about a marriage and a nasty divorce, and all the pieces clicked into place. Someone from here—a local guy—had hurt her, and in their minds, no one was ever going to do that again. Not on their watch. Even though I desperately wanted to know every single detail about her and this asshole ex, I never asked, forcing myself to act uninterested whenever the topic was brought up.

When I had first arrived in Port Rufton, I'd had no idea where I was headed. I'd packed up everything I needed to survive and just started driving up the interstate. All I knew was that I couldn't live in the city anymore. I had to get away from all the damage I'd caused before I drowned in it. I'd quit my job. Sold my house. Taken my dog, Barley, and bailed.

The weather had started beating down so badly that I could barely see the road in front of me. It was eerily reminiscent of the night I wanted so desperately to forget. To stop history from repeating itself, I ended up stopping and staying the night in the first town I drove up on. One night in Port Rufton was all it took.

I met a handful of locals who asked me way too many questions and refused to leave me alone, no matter how much I grumbled and complained. They fed me. Told me I looked like shit. And butted into my business, insisting that I stay here even if it was just temporarily. The storm wouldn't be letting up for a good four more days, and then the ice would set in. It wouldn't be safe to get on the road for at least another week. The next thing I knew, I was renting an old man's house along with his space at the dock and arranging to get my old fishing boat brought up to my new location as soon as possible.

I'd told myself it would only be for a little while, but I'd been here nine months already with no plans on leaving.

While I was still stuck in the past, Ava cleared her throat, bringing me firmly into the present. A smile lit up her whole face, and I felt mine frown in response. She let go of the coolers on the ground at her feet, and I gave Barley a warning to leave it. I knew by the time Ava reached me, her arms had to be getting tired of pulling all the weight, but she never complained. Or if she did, I never heard it.

"Morning, Tony," she said, and I gave her a gruff nod. I watched as her grin faltered before it reappeared. "Fish looks good," she complimented, perusing my stash.

"It was a good morning," I said as Barley betrayed me and walked under the table and right into Ava's legs.

She reached down to pet him before giving him a kiss on the nose.

"Barley, come," I demanded, and he slowly headed back to me and lay back down on his bed.

I didn't miss the disapproving look Ava shot my way, but I did ignore it.

"You caught oysters today?" she asked, sounding surprised.

It wasn't something I typically brought back with me, but they'd gotten caught up in my net somehow this morning, so I'd kept them instead of throwing them back.

"Only a handful," I mentioned, as if she couldn't see that information with her own eyes.

"I'll take them all."

"How were Bob's lobsters?" I found myself asking.

Ava looked like she'd won the damn lottery. I rarely initiated our conversations. Asked her questions even less often.

"They're huge! Have you seen them?"

"Not yet, but I heard all about them." I almost laughed, but I killed the sound in my throat before it could come out and give her the wrong impression.

"You have to check them out. They're unreal," she said before blowing out a soft breath. "I do hate when I have to cook them though."

She sounded so sad, and I'd never thought about it

before—what it took to create her famous lobster rolls.

"What do you mean?"

"Well, don't you feel bad when you catch the fish and they die?"

I gave her a half-hearted shrug. "I can't feel bad about that."

"What do you mean, you can't? Oh, because you have no feelings? No heart inside that chest of yours?"

I knew she was teasing as she stared right where my heart used to be. She was right. I didn't have one anymore, but admitting that to her would lead to a conversation I never planned on having.

"I can't feel bad about how I earn a living. And you shouldn't either." It was a scolding she didn't need, but I gave it to her anyway. "We're a damn fishing community. This entire town exists because of it. Without this ocean, we'd all starve to death."

It was a bit of an exaggeration, but there was also truth in what I'd said. Our jobs fed this town. There was a small market, of course, but if they went out of business tomorrow, we'd all live off the things we could grow and catch. Simple as that. This ocean sustained us.

"Well," she started to argue, her voice rising, "you think I don't know what we provide here? All I was saying was that I'm a woman. Killing things isn't natural to me. We're nurturers by nature."

"So, you don't feel bad about cooking the fish?" I glanced at her body, giving her a once-over from head to toe. The things I could do to her started flashing in my mind, and I shook my head to clear my thoughts.

"You already murder them for me. I have to do the dirty work myself when it comes to the lobsters." She visibly winced, as if cooking them caused her visceral pain. And honestly, it probably did, knowing her.

"You know that lobsters don't have brains, right? Brains are what allow us to process and feel pain." I was actually trying to be helpful, but my tone betrayed me, sounding the exact opposite.

"I know all of this, Tony. But they still do this little tail-twitch thing. No matter what I do to minimize their discomfort and quicken the process." She shuddered, her body jerking in response to the visual playing out in her mind.

"I think you might be in the wrong business, Ava."

"I think you might be right." She narrowed her eyes at me, and I wondered what I'd done.

If she quit and closed the restaurant, this town would never forgive me. I'd have to pack up and head out as quickly as I'd moved in, and I wouldn't blame them one bit.

INFURIATING AND SO DAMN HOT

AVA

TONY GARCIA WAS hands down the most frustrating man on the planet. Why was it so hard for him to have a normal conversation with me? Or to be actually kind whenever we spoke?

He hates me. That was the only logical explanation for his complete asshole behavior.

Then again, it wasn't like I'd seen him be friendly to other women here in town. But I had seen him smile before. Never at me, of course, but at least I knew his mouth could make the movement. I shouldn't be even remotely attracted to a man who wasn't nice to me, but here I was … dying to kiss the guy and run my fingers down his muscular chest.

What is wrong with me?

I'd literally learned nothing from my past. A good-looking guy did not equal a quality one. And being attracted to someone was merely that—a mixture of chemicals, lust, and maybe some good old-fashioned loneliness thrown in for extra measure.

There was something else there between us too even if I couldn't place it or give it a name. Something about Tony Garcia nagged at me, pulling and refusing to let go. It was like the universe didn't want me to give up on him—that was how it felt.

The faint tan line around his ring finger, which seemed to fade a little more each time I saw him, let me know that he had a past with someone, and it must not have been that long ago. And the way he'd shown up here with nothing but his truck and his dog said a lot too. Tony was a man starting over. Or one running away. I wasn't sure which, and I really wished I could stop caring what the correct answer was, but I was a curious creature.

I started heading toward the restaurant, lugging the heavy coolers, when I heard the pounding of feet running up behind me.

"Let me get those for you," the voice said, and I knew

it was Rory without even having to turn around.

Stopping, I let him take only one of them from my hands, his dirty-blond hair falling into his eyes.

"You don't have to do that, but thank you."

Rory and I had been friends forever. He used to be Liam's best friend, had even been the best man at our wedding, but after everything that had happened between us, Rory had picked a side ... and it wasn't Liam's. He was one of the few single guys in Port Rufton, and while I appreciated his friendship, I definitely didn't have any of those kinds of feelings for him.

"You should just ask everyone to drop off your deliveries, like I do. You know they will," he suggested.

I had thought about it briefly once, but my dad had never asked for special treatment, so I tried not to either.

I refused to swallow what little pride I had left and ask anyone for help or admit that I was still learning how to navigate certain details of running the shop on my own.

"I know. You guys are the best, but it's okay. I just need to come up with a better way. At least during tourist season."

Business tripled daily during the busy months, and I

needed far more food than I could carry on my own. I hadn't figured out how to handle all of the necessary details efficiently yet, but I knew I would.

"Just send one of your guys down to pick up the stuff while you start prepping for the day." Rory was just filled with all kinds of helpful ideas today.

"I would, but they're still sleeping." I gave a slight giggle.

My small staff didn't come in for another couple of hours.

"True," he grunted as soon as we started walking up hill. "This shit is way too heavy, Ava. I'm going to ask the guys to drop off your purchases each morning." I opened my mouth to complain, but he made a noise that stopped me. "Just during tourist season. I won't take no for an answer. And neither will they. It's not a big deal."

Before I could argue for no good reason at all, I relented. "If you're sure they won't mind. And only if it's okay with them. I can pay a little more for the delivery."

"Ava, stop," he said as we reached the back entrance to my kitchen.

I pulled out the keys from my pocket and unlocked the

door before holding it open with my hip for him to go in.

"We all love you. We'd do anything for you—you know that."

I did know that. "I hate asking for help," I whispered as he pulled the cooler past me and stopped next to the prepping station.

Being cheated on for over a year had been embarrassing. The fact that everyone here in Port Rufton had heard about it was even worse. I hated that people felt sorry for me because of it.

Rory wrapped an arm around my shoulders and tugged me against him in a tight hug before letting go. "We all do. But if the roles were reversed, you'd be banging down our doors, letting yourself in, not giving us a chance to say no." He laughed. "Tell me I'm wrong."

I only had to think for two seconds before agreeing with his assessment. "You're not wrong."

Pulling open one of the coolers, I started putting the wrapped pieces away. The ice wasn't set up to keep the fish chilled for very long. Rory started to help, and I knew asking him to stop would be pointless, so I allowed it, actually grateful.

"Can I ask you something?" He stood up tall, and I felt nerves shoot down my legs.

"Sure," I said, avoiding eye contact in case he asked what I thought he might.

"I like you, Ava," he started to say, and I swallowed hard, dreading what might come next.

Please don't ask me out. Please don't ask me out. Please don't ask me out, I silently chanted in my head.

I hated to hurt anyone's feelings, but I didn't want to lead Rory on either.

"Rory—"

He put up a hand to stop me. "No, let me finish. I like you. Always have. But I know you don't feel the same. It would be weird with the Liam thing anyway, right?" His mouth twisted up into a crooked grin, and I felt myself relax slightly. "But I do have a proposition for you."

Closing the refrigerator door, I gave him an inquisitive look. "What kind of proposition?" I asked before pushing the cooler lid shut tight while I listened.

"The kind that starts and ends with Tony Garcia."

Hearing him say Tony's name made me feel naked and exposed. Had my attraction to him been so obvious that everyone knew about it? Was I somehow the talk of the town again? How embarrassing.

"What about him?"

"The guy is so into you," he said, and I bent over as laughter escaped from my lips.

"You've got to be kidding," I tried to say, but I couldn't stop giggling. "He hates me."

Reaching for the cooler, I rolled it toward my legs and sat down on top of it. Rory did the same with the other, his body facing mine as our knees touched.

"You know men better than that." He gave me a knowing expression that told me that I should at least pretend to be more well versed in their behavior.

"What are you saying?"

"I'm saying that he likes you."

Shaking my head furiously, I disagreed, "He doesn't. You're wrong."

"You should see his face whenever one of us talks about asking you out," he said with a giant grin.

I realized that I had no idea what went on down at the wharf when I wasn't there. It never even occurred to me that I might be a topic of conversation between them.

I slapped his leg. "Stop it."

"I'm not kidding. We all do it. Every one of us."

"Even Bob?"

Bob was the oldest lobsterman on the water and had been married for fifty years. If he talked about asking me out, then Tony had to know it was a joke.

"Even Bob," he said before laughing again. "We do it just to mess with him, but he doesn't get it. He thinks we're all serious. He gets so worked up about it that we can't stop now."

He had my complete attention.

"What does he do? How does he act? You really think he gives a crap about me?"

"I knew you liked him too," he said, and I realized that I'd basically admitted exactly that with my rapid-fire questioning and hopeful tone.

"I shouldn't," I admitted.

"But you do. And it's okay." Rory reached for my face and held my chin in his hand.

"You really think he's interested?" I asked again, wanting to hear it one more time.

"Ava, he wants you so bad; it's written all over his

face. But for some reason, he won't go there. It has less to do with you and everything to do with him, I think. He won't tell us shit. We've asked. Tried to get to know him, but whatever he did before he came here, he won't let on."

"He was married at some point," I said softly, thinking about the tan line on his ring finger, and Rory nodded his head as he released his hold on my face.

"We've all gathered that much. But maybe it was like yours," he started to say before adding, "and it ended badly or something."

This all felt wrong somehow, talking about personal things behind Tony's back. Especially when we didn't know the truth and were basically gossiping about the man. I knew how crappy it felt to be the focal point when it was the last thing you wanted.

Clearing my throat, I stood up from my seat on top of the cooler. "So, where does this proposition come in?"

Rory stood up as well, his large frame looming over mine. "I'm going to ask you out in front of him, and you're going to say yes."

He looked so proud of himself, and I wondered if this was somehow a trick to get me to start dating him without realizing what I'd done.

"What will that do?"

"You'll see."

He stepped toward me and planted a kiss on my cheek right as Tony suddenly appeared at the back door, a murderous glare dancing in his eyes.

"You forgot these," he huffed out before dropping the wrapped oysters on the ground and storming away, cursing to himself as Barley followed in step behind his owner.

Tony had looked downright dangerous.

"Told you," Rory said with a pleased smile.

"So, now what?"

"We wait for Señor Grumpy Pants to admit his feelings to himself and come get his woman before someone else does," he said like it was all part of some master plan set in motion that couldn't be stopped anymore.

I was confused … by so many things. The look in Tony's eyes right then. Why Rory seemed to be so invested in the state of my heart.

"Why do you care so much? I mean, why are you doing this?"

He offered me a one-armed shrug before admitting,

"Because you deserve to be happy, Ava. I hate what Liam did to you, and I'm so sorry about it. I swear I didn't know." He sounded so sincere and concerned.

Since I'd been back in Port Rufton, we'd never really talked about what had happened. I'd been too embarrassed.

"I never thought you did," I said, and he looked relieved.

Not once had it ever crossed my mind that Rory might have known what his former best friend was doing behind my back. I had known it would have killed him to keep quiet and not tell me. I was grateful he'd never been put in that position.

"So, yeah ... you deserve happiness. And honestly, I hate seeing two people who so obviously like each other not give in to their feelings. Especially in this town," he continued, explaining why he was pushing me and Tony together.

"What are you saying?"

"That there aren't enough single people to go around, so it feels like a waste."

"Well now, I wouldn't want to be wasteful," I said

with a smile, and he nodded, like he had known I'd be agreeable.

"Once this works, by the way, you owe me."

He gave me a wink before heading out the back door, leaving me alone to finish loading up the fridge while *not* thinking about Tony Garcia and this plan.

THIS IS A BAD IDEA
AVA

M Y BEST FRIEND, Elise, was currently cracking up in my kitchen while I prepped today's menu and lunch specials before we opened.

"*He said what?* Oh, this is brilliant. I can't wait to watch it all unfold before my very eyes," she said as she rubbed her growing belly.

Elise and I had been friends since grade school. She had married the only guy she'd ever slept with and was pregnant with their first child. The two of them currently worked at one of the only inns in town. Everyone in Port Rufton seemed to inherit their family business if they stuck around long enough.

"You should have seen Tony's face when he saw Rory kiss my cheek. I thought he was going to burn the restaurant to the ground."

"Told you he likes you." She sounded so cocky about it all.

"Yeah, but you're supportive to a fault. I can't trust anything you say."

I gave her a look that dared her to disagree, and she grinned.

"You're not wrong. But I've been telling you since he first got here. That man wants a piece of you. And you should definitely give it to him."

Elise had been saying exactly those words since the moment Tony had arrived and stayed at her inn. The restaurant had been closed at the time since a big storm was heading in. I still cooked my meals there though and prepped a slew of deliveries for those who I knew wouldn't be able to get out of their homes once it hit.

I'd stopped by the inn to bring Elise some of my mom's desserts and a couple dozen cornbread muffins for any wayward guests or locals who wandered in. Apparently, Tony watched our interaction from the living room fireplace the entire time. I hadn't even seen him standing there. Elise claimed he was mesmerized. I told her she was insane. But then I had seen him for the first time a couple of weeks later, and it was me who had been damn near mesmerized.

"Do you think it's a bad idea?" I suddenly grew nervous as I replayed Rory's simple plan in my head.

"No. I think it's perfect. It's going to drive Tony mad." She clapped her hands together, and I wondered just how crazy pregnancy hormones made people.

"I'm not sure you're the best judge of things in your current state." I pointed toward her belly. "Get Greg on the phone. Let me ask him."

"Gladly." She reached for her cell and pressed a single button before setting it down on top of the counter. It started ringing out loud as we waited for him to pick up.

"How's my gorgeous wife and baby mama?" Greg answered, and we both grinned.

"Honey, I'm here with Ava," Elise said out loud. "And you're on speakerphone."

"Ohh. What'd I do? I didn't do it. I take it back. Don't double-team me!" he joked, and I shook my head.

Poor Greg had been dealing with our shenanigans for years.

"You're not in trouble," Elise said. "Unless you did

something. What'd you do?"

"Nothing, I swear." His voice turned instantly serious. "Ava, help me out."

"Nah, this is too much fun," I said.

"Honey, we called because Rory has a plan to help Ava," Elise started to explain before Greg cut her off.

"A plan with what? Getting revenge on Liam? Cutting off his dick? Making sure he gets an incurable STD? I'm in." He sounded so happy, joyful even at the idea of hurting Liam. "And I'd like to say, it's about damn time."

Elise shot me a look as she rolled her eyes. "You're the one who told me to call him."

I'd had no idea how invested people had become in the demise of my marriage. Or how much they hated Liam for what he'd done. Of course, Elise despised the guy—she was *my* best friend. But the way the men in town had reacted to the news when I first moved back was actually refreshing even though I was too traumatized at the time to truly appreciate it.

The men here in Port Rufton didn't think what Liam had done was cool. They called it inexcusable, and not even the age-old *typical guy behavior* line could get him off the hook. None of them defended him or his actions. Not even his parents. They had been ashamed and far more apologetic to me than Liam had been. As a matter of fact, I didn't think he'd ever said he was sorry, which was fine because I knew he wasn't.

"Hello? Are we doing this or what?" Greg asked, and the noise coming out of the speaker in the phone gave the impression that he was packing things in a hurry.

"It's not about dipshit Liam," Elise informed, and I heard Greg let out a disappointed groan, the background noise instantly stopping. "It's about hotshot Tony."

"Ah! Yes!" Greg's tone turned from sad to excited once more. "What about the hot new fisherman?"

Tony would always be considered the new guy. That was, until someone else moved here and took on the role.

"Rory has a plan to make him jealous, and Ava doesn't think it will work."

"That's not true," I argued. "I just wanted to know if it was a bad idea or not. From a guy's point of view."

"Well, what is it?" Greg asked, and we filled him in. It took literally five seconds to tell him the entirety of said *plan*. "Honestly, it's what I would suggest. I think Tony needs some kind of push. Even if it sends him over the edge."

I threw my head back with his words and blew out a breath toward the ceiling. "Over the edge?" I repeated, suddenly questioning everything.

"We don't want to throw the guy over any kind of edge, honey. We just want him to throw Ava into the sack." She tossed me a look. "Right?"

I started shaking my head. "I knew this wasn't good."

"Ava." Greg called my name like he knew I'd started pacing around the kitchen, and I stopped moving long enough for him to start talking again. "Sometimes, guys like Tony need to be tossed into the deep end without a floatation device, so they can learn how to swim."

"Are you seriously metaphoring me right now?" I asked, referring to the fact that men loved to use metaphors when explaining things to women. It was annoying.

"I'm just saying that if the guy thinks you'll wait around forever, he won't get off the pot. He'll watch from the sidelines, never tagging in because he doesn't have to."

"Oh my gosh," I groaned because … *more metaphors*

even though they were all mixed together and a jumbled mess.

"He needs a shove. And if he still doesn't do anything about it when he thinks he might lose his shot with you, then he doesn't deserve to have one."

"Damn, honey. That was hot," Elise said as she fanned her face with her hand.

"So," I interrupted their lovefest, "you're saying it's a good idea then?" I circled us back to the beginning and the point of the phone call in the first place.

Greg laughed. "It's a necessary evil, yes."

"Fine," I begrudgingly agreed and hoped like hell it worked.

LOSING MY DAMN MIND
TONY

THE FACT THAT I had arrived at Ava's back door just in time to see Rory plant a kiss on her cheek made me feel like the world was conspiring against me. It was a not-so-gentle reminder that feeling content could be ripped from my grasp at any moment. And even though I'd thought that I'd already accepted that fact, it'd still stung. Like a swift kick to the balls.

I shouldn't have been surprised to see them together. Rory had been warning me for weeks now that he was going to ask Ava out. And those threats had only grown more insistent in the recent days. He had literally spelled it out for me this morning in fact.

And now, I was standing here, stewing in anger, jealousy, and whatever other emotions were raging inside me. All because he had done what I'd sworn I never would.

"We good, man?" Rory was suddenly in front of me, his smug face just waiting for me to respond.

"Why wouldn't we be?" I snapped back.

He laughed, his stupid mouth grinning up in my direction. "Just asking since you practically punted whatever you brought for Ava onto the ground outside her door."

Shit.

He wasn't wrong about that. I had dropped her food at the sight of them together.

I glared at Rory, not giving two shits about his feelings or emotions about my actions from earlier, but if I'd upset Ava somehow, I'd hate myself even more for it—if that was even possible.

"Is she mad?"

"No," he responded, and even though I'd asked him the question, it still pissed me off that he knew the answer.

"So, you finally asked her? And she actually said yes?" Saying the words out loud was like swallowing glass— they stabbed and sliced and shredded my throat to pieces.

"Not yet, but soon. Gotta work my way up to it. Ease

Ava in, you know?"

I didn't know. I didn't know at all, but I didn't like it. Any of it. And I was tempted to admit as much to him, but there was no point.

"A woman like her can't stay single forever," he pushed, forcing me to confront things I had been trying my best to ignore. "Don't you agree? Someone is going to snag her up, and I'd kick myself if I didn't at least try to make that person me."

I mumbled something unintelligible and gave him a half-assed shrug, wishing he'd disappear and get the hell out of my sight. His words repeated in my head on a loop over and over again. The ones about her not staying single forever. The truth of them was like a two-by-four to the side of the head. Ava *was* a great catch, and the whole damn town knew it.

I'd always sensed it.

And while Ava dating someone from here was something I'd thought about at least a hundred times over the past nine months, a part of me never considered it an actual threat. The idea of her with some local guy wasn't rooted in reality. If she wanted one of them, wouldn't she already have them? She always kept her distance from most of the guys and treated us all with the same level of kindness and compassion. At least, that was how I'd always read her.

I looked up to see Rory still standing in front of me for some reason. "What are you waiting for then?" The words tumbled from my mouth before I could stop them, and I knew that I was either going to be right with my Ava assessment or this was going to blow up in my face big time.

Rory looked a little surprised, his surfer-looking blond hair hanging over his eyes before he scooped it all back and tucked it inside a baseball cap with his fishing logo on it. "You're right."

"I know," I agreed even though I had no idea what the hell I was agreeing with.

He started nodding his head like he was having a full-on conversation that only he could hear. The guy was probably trying to psych himself up to go through with it.

"I'm going to do it."

"Good for you."

"Today!" he practically shouted.

Barley stood up, his tail wagging, and I pushed on his backside to make him sit back down. Barley was only allowed to get riled up for me. Not the enemy here.

"Today?" I almost choked on the word.

"Yeah. You're right. I just need to do it and stop waiting. I'm going to ask her later. At her restaurant."

Rory continued to talk out loud, his plan spilling out all over the table between us, his tone rising with his excitement, and I pretended to act like this didn't affect me at all.

"Sounds good." I started moving some of my fish from the ice trays to a cooler.

If Rory would get out of my space, I could pack up my things and head home to pout in private.

"Wait a second." Rory blew out a breath through his nose, his eyes narrowing. "Why are you encouraging me to do this?"

"Because I don't think there's a chance in hell she'll tell you yes." I grinned like the asshole I was.

"Seriously?"

"What? Am I wrong?"

"I sure as hell hope so," he said as he stuffed his hands

in the pockets of his shorts before yanking them out again.

"I guess we'll find out later," I offered.

His eyes practically bugged out of his head. "What do you mean?"

"Oh, buddy. I wouldn't miss this for anything." I laughed before he shut me right up.

He took a small step closer to me and lowered his voice. "You know, you're going to be sorry. You're going to be sitting there, wishing it were you, knowing that it probably could have been but that you were too chickenshit to ask and find out. So, instead of it being your body keeping Ava's warm in her bed, it's going to be mine. And you're going to hate every second of it because you'll always know that it might have been different if you'd only tried. You'll have to live with that fact every single day."

His words struck more than a single nerve in me. It hit them all.

"You have no idea what I have to live with every single day, Rory. No fucking idea," I spat before I turned my back on him and packed up the rest of my shit in a fury.

"You're right. I don't. But I'm pretty sure you deserve to be happy. Even if you don't think you do."

I tried my best to ignore him and not respond, so when I looked back over my shoulder, I was grateful to find Rory across the way at his station, no longer paying me any attention.

He had no idea what he was talking about, and he couldn't have been more wrong. Happiness was the last thing I deserved. I'd had it once. And then I'd lost it. No, I'd destroyed it.

I WAS CURRENTLY sitting in my house, staring at the wall, my hand absentmindedly rubbing Barley's head as I tried my best not to come unglued. I'd been sitting here for hours. There was so little holding me together right now that I figured I could unravel at any moment. I hadn't felt this out of control in a long time. My past always lingered close behind, but I'd gotten good at keeping it at bay and attempting to live a normal life. Even if I was alone for the rest of it.

Meeting Ava had thrown me all out of whack. She was

such a bright and beautiful light that it emanated from her very being, and it had pulled at me the first time I ever laid eyes on her at the inn. But I had been in such a dark place that I couldn't risk the chance of snuffing it out, certain that I had nothing to offer her other than the pitch-black hole I was living in.

Not much had changed in nine months. I was still a rain cloud, and she was still the sun.

Thinking about her made me smile without warning. I thought about Rory's plan and realized that Ava was far too sweet to ever tell him no, especially if he asked her out in front of other people. She'd never embarrass him like that. Even if she didn't want to go, she'd agree in order for him to save face.

But what if she didn't?

There had to be sides to Ava I hadn't figured out yet. Pieces of her that I had no idea existed. She'd been hurt in the past. Cheated on, I'd overheard in passing once. That kind of thing had to change a person. Yet here Ava was, still hopeful, kind, and warm.

I had it bad for the woman. Couldn't even see a single negative quality about her. And worst of all, Rory knew it.

He had damn well called me out on it. Practically dared me to challenge him for her affection.

I sat up straight.

"He told me to challenge him," I said out loud, still stroking Barley's head when he moved to look at me, his ears perking up. "What do you think, boy? Why would Rory want me to fight him for the same girl?"

Barley whined in response, his tail thumping against the couch.

"You're right. He has some kind of angle. You're so smart," I complimented my dog, who I'd grown to believe could communicate with me with looks and head tilts.

Rory had said that I deserved to be happy. It was an odd thing for a man to say to another man … especially when you didn't really know each other.

Why would he have said that? I wondered.

Reaching for my cell phone, I pulled up my *mami*'s contact information and debated on texting her. I knew that she would call me in response instead of writing back, and I wasn't sure that I was up for a heavy conversation right now. She always asked too many questions.

If I told her about Ava, she'd probably get on the next

flight from Puerto Rico, just to play matchmaker. Maybe that was what I was secretly searching for—permission to try. I could hear her in my head now, telling me to run to Ava's restaurant and tell her that Rory was all wrong for her. That any man in this town who wasn't me was all wrong for her. Then, *Mami* would encourage me to take Ava in my arms and kiss the sense right out of her. *Mami* loved her telenovelas, got all of her romance advice from them. I'd grown up watching them with her, too, so I understood her obsession completely.

She always ended our calls by reminding me that what had happened wasn't my fault. I wished I could believe her. I wanted to—I really did—but some part of me refused to let myself off the hook that easily. I'd hurt far too many people.

Mami would tell me that a man without love in his life was like a day without sun. She would remind me how much I'd always loved the sun, claimed I couldn't live without it as a kid. Then, she'd tell me how much she loved me, and I would tell her she didn't need to worry about me anymore. She worried anyway. I hated that I was the cause.

Barley hopped off the couch and barked twice, heading for the front door.

"What is it, boy?" I asked as I followed his lead.

Rory.

He was walking in the direction of Ava's restaurant. To be fair, most of the town was in the same direction, but he looked like a man on a mission. I'd never seen him so cleaned up before. From this view, his hair even looked like it was styled.

I glanced down at Barley and knew I couldn't stay here, feeling sorry for myself anymore. I was either going to sit in Ava's place and watch Rory ask her out in front of everyone or I was going to do it myself before he ever got the chance. There wasn't any time to waste.

Blowing out a breath, I mumbled to myself before heading out the door and stalking down the hill.

If Ava Starling was going to be with anyone in this town, it was going to be me. End of story.

WHEN YOUR PAST WALKS THROUGH THE DOOR

AVA

T HE RESTAURANT WAS hopping, almost every seat and table spoken for with the exception of a few empty stools at the bar. I was grateful, but I was also exhausted. Most of the kitchen staff had been with us for years, so I leaned on them more than I thought my dad ever had. But like I'd mentioned before, I was still learning how to manage it all on my own without losing it all in the process.

Glancing around at the cooks, I gave them a nod before taking off my apron and pushing through the swinging double doors. I liked to meander through the small space, checking on guests and chatting with the locals. The food still got cooked to perfection without me standing over the stove every second. I trusted my men in the kitchen to do their respective jobs right; they'd been doing it long before I ever moved back home.

The bell over the front door gave a quick jingle, drawing my attention toward it, and I watched as Rory stepped inside, looking all dressed up.

I rushed over to him, my eyes widening. "You look so nice."

I grinned, and he gave me a hug.

"Don't have to sound so surprised about it," he whispered in my ear, and I nodded in agreement.

It was supposed to be a compliment, but it had sort of come out sounding a little backhanded.

"You're right. I'm not. It's just been a while since I've seen you without a hat," I said, trying to recover. "Anyway, are you staying for dinner?" I asked, and he slapped his hands together and rubbed them back and forth.

That was when it hit me—exactly why he was here, looking all put together and dapper. Rory's plan had begun. I had no idea why I stood there, feeling so shocked in my realization, but that was the emotion that took over my body. Well, that, and a little fear.

We'd only talked about the idea this morning, and now, it was already happening tonight? In front of all these people?

I really hadn't thought this through.

"You okay?" Rory asked, and I blew him off before leading him toward an empty seat at the bar.

"It's all we have."

He grinned. "It's all I need."

"But Tony's not even here." I leaned toward him, hoping he wouldn't put me on the spot if our person of interest never showed.

"Yet. He's not here yet," he said with confidence as the bartender, Jin, walked over and took his drink order.

"Need anything, boss?" Jin asked.

I made a silly face. He knew I rarely drank and never on the clock.

"I'm good, thanks."

"Just thought I'd check. You never know. These tourists can drive anyone to drink." He threw his head back like he couldn't wait for the season to finally end.

"These tourists pay our bills for the entire year," I said even though he already knew that.

Everyone in Port Rufton knew that the out-of-towners, no matter how difficult they could be at times, kept us afloat during those winter months when we were forced to stay closed. Half the businesses in town shut their doors completely from November to February. The weather was simply too unpredictable to stay open with any regularity, and getting supplies was even more difficult. I, however, tried my best to keep the restaurant going, but with limited hours. It seemed to work. And it kept the town fed.

"Oh shit." Rory suddenly grabbed me by the waist and spun me around just in time to see my ex-husband, Liam, walking through the front door, a determined look on his face.

"Why on earth …" I started to question, but the words died on my lips as his eyes searched the room before landing on mine and holding.

"Did you know he was in town?" Rory asked as people began whispering around us at the bar.

The tourists had no idea what was going on, thankfully, but the handful of locals all knew exactly what was happening.

"We got your back, Ava," one of the guys said from

his seat at the opposite end of the bar.

I forced a smile in return right as Liam stopped in front of me, his eyes glaring with disapproval.

"Knew I'd find you here. Right where I left you."

Seriously? Where he left me?

"If you remember correctly, I left you. Back in the city. What do you want?"

Liam looked around, as if taking stock or inventory on a place that no longer had anything to do with him. "Nice to see what my money has given you."

"Given me?" I practically spat in his face.

My family had done this for me, not Liam or any of his adulterous dollars.

"You think I don't notice the upgrades? New floor. Updated signage. Who knows what you've added in the kitchen."

He tried to look around my shoulder toward the swinging double doors, but Rory stood tall behind me, blocking his view. It wasn't like he could see inside of there anyway. He would have to walk into the space, and no one here would ever let that happen.

"Why are you here, Liam?" Rory asked, and Liam's

eyes practically lit up, as if he had only just noticed him.

"Oh man. You're joking, right? Please tell me you two are not together. That would just be rich," Liam asked with a sick-sounding laugh.

Before I could answer, Tony was suddenly at my side, asking if everything was okay and attempting to break the tension.

I hadn't even heard or seen him come in, although my body was hyperaware of his nearness. With my attention zeroed in on Tony's broad shoulders and dark eyes, my response to his question died in my throat with one word from Liam.

"Tony?"

I watched as Tony turned, as if in slow motion, meeting my ex-husband's curious gaze with one of his own. "Liam?"

"What are you doing here?" they both asked one another at the same exact time.

I looked between the two men, my confusion crystal clear.

"You two know each other?" I pointed between them as my world started to spin.

Bracing myself on the back of one of the barstools, I suddenly felt sick. *How the hell does Liam know Tony?*

"Unfortunately," Tony bit out, his tone disgusted, and that at least gave me a small sliver of joy.

If they were acquainted somehow, it wasn't necessarily a good thing. My stomach settled slightly.

Liam scoffed at Tony's response before adding his own. "Thanks for leaving the firm, by the way," he said, his tone smug and arrogant.

"Let me guess. They gave you my job?" Tony sounded completely uninterested and unimpressed.

If I'd thought I couldn't be more intrigued by the man, I was wrong. Color me nothing but intrigued.

"I earned your job, fuck you very much." Liam sounded like a snotty brat.

He was nothing like the guy I'd fallen in love with all those years ago. That person was long gone.

"You always were a little bitch," Tony whispered harshly under his breath, trying his best not to create a scene.

Liam shifted on his feet before he leaned toward Tony to deliver a final blow. "Yeah? Well, at least I didn't kill my wife," Liam said loud enough for those around to start paying attention, and I released a surprised gasp.

Tony killed his wife? What exactly does that even mean?

"No. You just cheated on yours until she finally got some sense and left you," Tony zinged back before the situation and the realization of what'd he just said hit him somehow. He whirled to the side, his focus solely on me. "It was you?" he asked softly. "You were married to him?"

"Don't feel bad for her. She took half of everything."

Tony whipped his head back toward Liam. "She should have taken it all. Stay the hell away from her." His tone was threatening, and my heart raced. It was the most emotion I'd ever seen from Tony.

"Or what? You'll kill me too?" Liam asked with a grin that begged Tony to take this further.

Tony took a step toward him, his hands balled into fists, but Rory was right there, holding him back. He said something that I couldn't quite make out, but it seemed to work. Tony's fists unfurled.

"You got this?" he asked Rory.

With an affirmative nod, Tony took off toward the

back exit and out the door, and I watched him disappear.

Rory convinced Liam he needed to leave. The group of locals who were standing like a pack of guard dogs, just waiting for the order to attack, probably helped sway his decision. This wasn't a fight that Liam had any chance of winning.

As soon as Liam was out the front door, Rory turned to face me. "Go. He needs you," he said.

We both knew exactly which man he was referring to. I only hoped that he would let me inside.

YOU CAN NEVER RUN FAR
ENOUGH AWAY
TONY

I WAS WALKING as fast as my legs would take me without breaking into a jog before I decided to slow the hell down. There was no reason for me to run home. My heart—the one thing I hadn't thought I even had anymore—was pounding inside my chest so hard, begging to break free.

Coming to Port Rufton had been nothing but an escape at first. I'd been running away at the time, from everyone and everything I'd ever known, trying my damnedest to leave it all behind and numb the pain. Operating in survival mode was all I could manage after I lost it all. *Killed it all*, was actually more accurate.

Port Rufton had started to feel like a real home. It had become a place I never planned on leaving. At least, not anytime soon. But Liam showing up here today had destroyed any semblance of peace that I'd actually began to build.

I'd been able to have a new life even if it was a solitary one. A life where my past was slowly settling into where it belonged and me hating myself lessened just the tiniest bit each morning. Seeing his face had brought it all back. And his presence was like blowing up a jigsaw puzzle and watching all the pieces scatter after you finally completed it. Only the pieces were my sanity … my well-being.

All blown to bits.

"Tony!"

Ava.

I should have known that she'd follow me. She was the last person I wanted to see right now, but she was also the only person I could stomach. Barely.

"Tony. Stop!" she shouted, and I knew it was no use.

If I didn't, she'd follow me all the way home and force her way inside. Knowing Barley, he'd probably let her in.

"What do you want, Ava?"

Jesus. Even when I so desperately needed her to not think badly of me, I was pushing her away. My defense mechanism was one hell of an asshole.

"I want to talk to you," she said softly as she reached me, her hazel eyes glassy. Had she been crying? "About what Liam said back there." She thumbed in the direction of her restaurant, but I knew what she meant without the added gesture.

My skin prickled as I thought of Liam and his words. How harshly he'd said them. The fire inside me raged. I was embarrassed. Broken. Humiliated.

"Please," she begged sweetly, and I knew that I couldn't deny her. Not anymore. Not after today.

I still couldn't believe that she was the woman who used to be married to that little prick. A long breath escaped my lungs, and I thought my body might deflate into nothing but a pile of bones. I'd been holding it all in for so long now, afraid that once I started admitting the truth, saying it all out loud, I might never be able to stand on my own two feet again.

"Okay," was all I managed to get out.

When she reached for my hand, I let her take it, reveling in the contact.

It had been too long since I'd let anyone touch me. I

understood that now.

When we reached my front door, I twisted the knob, knowing it would open. I rarely locked it once I was off my boat for the day. Barley was at our feet in an instant, wagging his tail and rubbing his head against Ava's legs.

I watched as she looked around the space, her hand petting Barley's head absentmindedly. The house had come fully furnished, and in the nine months since I'd been here, I'd changed and added very little.

"Are you all right?" she asked me when I should have been the one making sure that she was.

Her ex had shown up here and created a scene. Even though I hated what he'd said to me, I hadn't been the point of his visit; Ava was. At least, that was what I assumed.

"Me? Are you?" I asked before sitting down on the couch and directing her to take a seat as well.

"Seeing Liam was"—she paused as she sat, searching for the right word—"unexpected. And definitely unwanted."

Barley followed her every step. He moved in between her legs on the floor at her feet, wanting her attention. Or maybe he sensed that she needed comforting. Whichever one it was, it worked. She grinned at him before scratching behind his ear.

"You had no idea he was in town?" I asked, and she shook her head.

"I haven't seen him since I left." She stopped petting Barley and leaned into the chair, her head resting against the padded back. "His parents still live here, so I should have expected that he'd come back home at some point. I don't know." She stumbled on her thoughts. "I just didn't."

"I get it. He could have come to town without going into your restaurant," I said, my voice rising as I realized how big of a jerk the guy truly was. "He did that on purpose."

"I know," she agreed.

"Any idea why?"

Her eyes held mine. "Because he thought it would hurt me?" she asked, so I knew she had no idea either and was simply offering up a guess.

"Did it?" I wondered out loud. "Hurt you, I mean?"

"No. Six months ago, it might have. But not anymore."

I still couldn't believe that sweet, gentle, full-of-light Ava had been married to that piece of shit. He'd been screwing his assistant for years behind her back, seemingly proud of that fact. He used to brag about it all the time. I remembered thinking how young and stupid he was. That cheating on your wife wasn't a badge of honor and, one day, he'd realize that. Until then, I'd hoped he'd get caught. Guys like him deserved to.

"I can't believe you were married to him. I'm sorry for what I said," I apologized, hoping that I hadn't embarrassed her with my harsh words.

She folded her hands in her lap as Barley rested his head on her thigh.

Lucky dog.

"You said the truth."

"I didn't realize I was talking about you though."

"I know."

I shifted on the couch, uncomfortable in every way. "I gotta ask you something, Ava."

"Okay."

"How in the world did you end up with a guy like that?" I didn't mean to be offensive or cruel, but the second I asked the question, I wanted to take it back.

Thankfully, Ava didn't look upset. It was almost as though she'd expected me to ask.

"He wasn't always like that," she explained. "That guy back there? I don't even recognize him anymore."

It was the only thing that made sense. Because I couldn't picture her with someone so deceptive and unkind.

"He used to be nice?" I asked, my tone showing I was unwilling to believe it.

The Liam I knew was cutthroat and willing to step on anyone in order to get ahead. It wasn't atypical in our industry, especially for someone his age, but he seemed more intent than most who had come before him. He always acted like he had nothing to lose.

Ava nodded her head slowly. "I thought so. We started dating back in high school. He was such a different guy then. Quieter, you know?" She looked like she was remembering a simpler time, a time I couldn't even imagine, much less picture. "He was still determined and wanted to be successful, but not at any cost, the way he is now."

A cough escaped from somewhere deep in my throat, and Ava shot me a look.

"Sorry," I said, putting up a hand. "It's just that the man I knew was willing to do anything to succeed."

"I learned that eventually. But up until that point, I was pretty naive. I trusted him. And I stupidly believed that love could conquer all."

"It's not stupid to think that," I said without a second thought, and I could tell that I surprised her. "You were just with the wrong person."

A small laugh escaped from her delicate lips. "You think so?" she asked.

"I know so."

"I guess love doesn't stop you from cheating." The words were followed by a long exhale, and I wondered if she knew the details of his infidelity or not.

"You knew about his affair?"

"I found out," she said, swallowing hard before her beautiful eyes narrowed in my direction. "Wait. You knew about it?"

I hated admitting this part to her. It felt too personal. Too none of my business, but I couldn't lie. Wouldn't lie.

"I knew. Everyone in the office knew," I said, clearly adding insult to injury.

"That's so embarrassing." She avoided eye contact, and I completely understood why she felt that way even though I hated that she did.

"It is, but not for you," I tried to reassure her. "When I tell you that he was the one who looked like a dick, I mean it."

Aside from a few guys who had high-fived his exploits, the rest had known it would blow up in his face eventually. But guys like Liam had to learn the hard way.

"Still," she said, "his assistant. It's so cliché."

"It is," I agreed.

"I hate that he showed up here, dredging up all these feelings," she said out loud, and I wasn't sure if she was talking to herself or me. "I had him neatly tucked away in a box. And now, it feels like I'm back at square one, if that makes any sense."

It made too much sense. Seeing Liam here, a part of the life I'd left behind, dredged things up for me too.

"I get it completely. He's done some damage here too." I tapped the side of my head with my finger.

Her eyes softened, and I knew what was coming. "Can I ask about your wife?"

This was the part I'd been dreading the most. There was no way to avoid it. Not after what Liam shouted for everyone to hear and interpret how they saw fit. But I hadn't been ready for it.

Then again, was anyone ever prepared to talk about how they had killed their wife?

LEARNING THE TRUTH
AVA

"**D**ON'T YOU NEED to get back to the restaurant?" Tony asked, and I knew he wanted to avoid this topic of conversation, but I wasn't letting him off the hook that easily.

Tony and I had found ourselves on some sort of common ground, and I'd be damned if I walked away from it. Not yet. Not when doing so would give him the time to build his walls back up and pretend like he didn't want to cross this line with me.

I saw it in his eyes—the interest and the desire. Glancing at the old clock on the wall, I couldn't believe I'd been at his house for well over an hour already. Tony and I had never been in each other's presence for this long before.

"I do, but not yet."

"You're sure?"

"Tony ..." I said his name softly and noticed the way it relaxed him.

His shoulders dropped before tightening back up.

"We were at a business event," he started to explain before his eyes pulled together with the memory. "Liam was there. You weren't though. I would have remembered meeting you." His head shook. "Lydia—she was my wife." He said her name with a smile, and my heart ached for him. "She wasn't feeling well, but she was always willing to take one for the team. Know that saying?" he asked, and I nodded. "God, she said it all the time. She truly was a team player and would do anything to help me. That included going to my boring work events when she felt like shit."

"She sounds really great." It slipped out, my assessment of his apparent dead wife, but it was the truth. She sounded like a nice person. My words hurt him though. I saw it all over his face.

He shifted on the couch, like he was suddenly uncomfortable in his own skin and wished he could get out of it.

"She was selfless."

He grew quiet, and I stared at him, watching his chest move in and out with each breath he took. I wanted to hear more, everything honestly, but pushing him too hard on this felt wrong.

His dark eyes met mine, and it took everything in me to stay seated in the chair and not rush to his side. I wanted to take him in my arms, tell him everything would be okay, and just … hold him. He looked like he needed it.

"Like I said, she wasn't feeling well, so she asked if we could go."

I leaned forward, put my elbows on my knees, and listened intently. The words were spilling so slowly from his lips; it was almost torturous. A better person might have told him to stop, that he didn't need to go on and relive this moment, but I was obviously not that person. He was opening himself up to me, and I wanted to reach inside his armor with both hands and hold on for dear life.

"The weather was shit outside. One of those nights where it was a mix between rain and snow with ice in patches. She apologized for wanting to leave," he said with a gruff laugh. "Can you believe that? She was telling me she was so sorry that she didn't feel good. I put my hand on her forehead, and she was burning up. Must have had at least a hundred-degree fever. She was so hot. And I was looking at her, letting her know that the event didn't matter. I just wanted her to be okay. I was focused on her and not on the road. I just"—he paused for a moment, as if he could see her face clearly in his mind—"couldn't stop staring at her."

I had no idea what might be coming next. Obviously, I sensed that there had been an accident, but the details eluded me. I held my breath as I waited for him to continue.

"The car started slipping. I wasn't even paying attention. And by the time I looked away from Lydia and back at the road, it was too late. I lost control. Hit a patch of black ice, and there was nothing I could do. I tried though. I tried so damn hard to keep us on the pavement," he said, his voice breaking.

"We rolled down an embankment and hit a tree. That tree stopped us from continuing even farther down the hill. The only reason the car stopped rolling was because of it. That tree broke our fall, but it's also why my wife died.

The impact of hitting it was on her side, and a branch broke through the window, and …" He sucked in a ragged breath before finishing his sentence.

"Tony," I breathed out, my eyes filled with water.

He could stop now. This was too much for him to relive, and I felt almost guilty for wanting him to share this with me. He still loved the woman he'd lost. He probably always would.

"Don't, Ava. Don't say it wasn't my fault. I killed my wife because I couldn't fucking stop staring at her."

Snapping my lips shut, I debated on staying quiet or not, but the way he blamed himself was too much.

"It was an accident. It could have happened even if you were watching nothing but the road."

"I'm not sure I believe that," he argued, and I'd known he would. Tony was the kind of guy to take responsibility and wear it like a straitjacket. "I didn't protect her. I didn't keep her safe. I took my eyes off the road, and it killed her."

He bent in half, his hands covering his face, and I watched as his large frame started to shake. This strong man was losing it in front of me, and I knew he'd hate himself for it later. It was the last thing I wanted. Pushing up from the couch, I scooted toward his body and wrapped my arms around his middle and held on tight.

He reached for me then, burying his head against my body as he pulled me onto his lap, his body still slightly convulsing. It might have looked awkward from the outside, the way we were twisted up with one another, but I wouldn't have stopped for anything. Tony was letting me comfort him.

I rubbed his back with one hand and gripped him hard with the other. He eventually stilled in my arms, and I wondered if the headiness of the moment was weighing down on him. His body disconnected from mine, his head moving away from my chest, and he looked at me, a mixture of so many emotions in his gaze.

"I'm sorry," he breathed out, his eyes oscillating between my own and my mouth.

I shouldn't have wanted to kiss him in that moment, but it was all I thought about.

"For what?" I asked.

"For what I'm about to do," he answered.

Before I could question him again, his lips were on

mine. My entire body melted into his. Just a few seconds ago, I'd been holding him together, but now, he was clearly the one holding me in place.

His kiss was soft and hard, all at once. Possessive and punishing. He breathed into me, against me, sounds coming from somewhere deep inside of him that only made me want him more. His hand gripped me firmly as his tongue explored my mouth, claiming every inch of space. And just as quickly as it had begun, it stopped.

Tony hopped up from the couch, taking my body with him, and separated himself from me. He took a few steps back and held his hand in the air to stop me from approaching. "Shit, Ava. I shouldn't have done that," he said, and he took all the wind out of my sails.

I loved that he'd done that. I wanted him to do it again.

"You're allowed to move on," I said and instantly knew it was the wrong thing to say by the way his expression shifted into something resembling anger.

"You need to leave," he demanded, and I stood firmly in place. "Now, Ava. Go."

And just like that, I'd ruined the moment. There would be no going back. So, I did as he'd asked without complaint or another word.

SHIT, SHIT, SHIT
TONY

*W*HAT THE HELL *was I thinking?*

I'd practically mauled Ava's face, not even giving her a chance to say she didn't want it, before I was all over her, taking that perfect mouth with mine. Kissing her was like bathing in the sun—you wanted it to cover you completely.

It was the first moment of true joy I'd felt since Lydia died. Which was why I stopped giving in to it. In that brief respite, I wasn't thinking about how badly I felt about the accident or the fact that my wife was dead because I was a piss-poor driver.

Even though I'd just been talking about exactly that, it all disappeared the moment my lips touched Ava's. My only thoughts were of her and how damn good she tasted. And how I wanted more of her ... *all* of her. My mind instantly went to the bedroom, and I imagined us there, her body naked beneath mine as we made love.

Guilt poured through me.

How could I have been crying over my dead wife one second and thinking about sleeping with another woman in the next? What kind of person did that? *A monster*—that was who.

I was filled with so much self-loathing when Ava told me that I was allowed to move on. My gut reaction was to get pissed, defensive. Logically, my brain knew that she was right. Of course she was. But emotionally, her words stung like sharp razor blades to the flesh. Maybe I didn't want to move on. Had she ever thought about that? Moving on meant letting go, and that wasn't something I was willing to do.

I'd basically kicked her out of the house. Honestly, I'd expected more of a fight out of her, but when she didn't give it, I felt like shit. Barley followed her to the front door and was currently staring out of it, no doubt watching her go.

A part of me knew I should be chasing after her, but the rest of me craved the solitude. I needed a moment to recover. To process everything that I'd admitted and the feelings I'd given in to. And honestly, what it all meant.

I probably should have started packing my things right then and there to hightail it out of town, but I didn't. I stayed put.

THE NEXT MORNING, I didn't fish. I tried to sleep in, but my body refused, waking me up well before the sun, like usual. When I couldn't sit in bed, watching TV, any longer, I got up, made some coffee and eggs, and grabbed Barley's leash.

If Ava had noticed my absence down at the marina, she didn't let on. I guessed I'd half-expected her to show up at my front door, demanding to know where I was. She seemed like the type.

Barley and I walked in the opposite direction of the water, hoping to avoid anyone who might ask too many questions. That was the thing about really small towns—keeping people out of your business was hard. Everyone wanted to know e-v-e-r-y-t-h-i-n-g, and they didn't hesitate to stick their noses in it, so to speak. I had no doubt that the majority of people had heard about Liam being back and what he'd said by now. Word traveled lightning fast here.

"Tony, is that you?" a man's voice called out in the distance.

I groaned to myself before giving Barley a look. This was exactly what I didn't need. I really shouldn't have left the cottage at all. Barley would have been fine with running around the small yard.

"Morning," I said as Barley and I approached Mr. and Mrs. Stanley.

They used to run the post office in town, but they were retired now.

"Why aren't you at the docks? You feeling okay?" Mr. Stanley asked before the missus interrupted.

"Of course he's not okay. We heard about what happened last night. Pity about your wife," she said as she leaned toward me, clearly wanting more information on the subject.

But I'd had enough sharing to last me a while.

"Thanks for saying that." I tried to be polite, but it was a struggle.

Barley nudged my leg with his nose, and I gave him a pat.

"You didn't really *murder* her, did you?" she asked, tripping on the word like it had gotten stuck to her tongue on the way out.

"Depends on who you ask, I suppose," I said with a shrug, and Mrs. Stanley gasped.

It was a shit response, but it felt like the truth.

The crash had been ruled an accident by the police, and I wasn't charged with reckless driving even though I would have understood it if I had been. My blood alcohol level was 0.0. I hadn't had a single drink at the party, so I knew I wasn't drunk, but it was standard procedure for them to check.

Lydia's parents were devastated, and her dad blamed me, saying more than once that I'd killed his baby girl. I knew that he needed someone to be angry with, and I was the only one still living who fit the bill. He couldn't be mad at the ice on the road, or the tree, or God, so he chose me instead. And I had taken it willingly because I agreed completely that it was all my fault.

"Of course he didn't murder his wife. Stop asking

nonsense, woman!" Mr. Stanley snapped before apologizing to me on her behalf. "One last thing," he started to say, and my body tensed as I waited. "Liam's a real piece of work. Used to be a nice kid. Not sure what happened there, but we're all Team Ava around these parts."

"Okay." I wasn't sure what the point of his commentary was.

"Just saying that none of us would miss him if he never came back around," he added, and I was still just as clueless to his meaning.

"Are you hinting at Tony to kill the man?" his wife asked.

I shot Mr. Stanley a look because ... *is he???*

"Good gracious, woman, pipe down. I'm not telling you to whack him. Just telling you that we don't like him. And we like Ava. And Ava clearly likes you. So, you're okay in my book."

"Why didn't you just say that then?" the missus asked, her tone agitated. "He's always beating around the bush instead of coming right out and saying what he means."

"I do not." He fought back.

She leaned toward me once more, her hand cupping her mouth. "He does. But he's right. Ask her out already. We're all waiting, and we're getting old."

What?

See what I mean about small towns?

"I'll think about it," I said with a forced smile, way past my comfort level at this point.

Before the two of them could give me any more unwanted advice, I gave them a wave and tugged at Barley's leash to get him moving.

All I wanted to do was get back to my place and lock myself inside. Which was why the shadow I saw standing at my front door was the last person I wanted to be around at the moment.

Rory.

"Hey, man," he said, his face etched with something more than concern.

"Why are you here?" I asked, unhooking Barley and opening the door for him. He leaped inside, and I heard him splashing in his water bowl, no doubt making a huge mess on the floor that I'd have to clean up.

"I just came to make sure you were all right."

"I don't need a babysitter."

"You don't always have to be such a dick, man. You have friends here whether you realize it or not."

He thought we were friends? He was my competition. My adversary. Not my friend.

"Listen," he continued even though I hadn't said anything, "you weren't at the docks this morning. Liam called you a fucking murderer. And when Ava finally came back to the restaurant last night, she was crying."

That got my attention.

My eyes swung to his. "She was crying?"

"She pulled it together pretty quick, but, yeah, she was crying. I just came by to make sure you hadn't bailed on her without at least saying good-bye."

"I'm not going anywhere," I said and felt my resolve kick into high gear.

The realization shocked me. After everything that had gone down last night, I still didn't want to leave Port Rufton. Not for good anyway.

This was my home now.

"Super."

I reached for the hat on my head and pulled it off. "I

don't get you."

Rory laughed. "How so?"

"You want Ava, but you're here, telling me not to leave her. What's your angle?"

"I care about her. But for whatever reason, she cares about you more."

My competitive side liked hearing that a whole lot. But there was more to it than that. Something warm and foreign coursed through my body when I thought about Ava actually choosing me. I realized I liked the idea. It was what I wanted. Even if I didn't deserve it.

"Try not to screw it up," he said with a grin before adding, "and in case you're wondering, which I know you are, Liam left town already. And Ava definitely noticed your absence this morning. I'd make it right before you give that poor girl a heart attack. You have her number, yeah?"

I wasn't even sure how it had happened at the time, but I did have her phone number.

"Yeah."

"Use it," he directed before turning to leave, his mission accomplished. "Oh, I almost forgot." He reached into his pocket and held up a ball of paper. "Here's a list of things she loves. I'm sure you can figure out what to do with it."

He tossed it in my direction, and I caught it easily before unfolding it, seeing a few different items written down.

"Hey, Rory," I said, and he faced me. "Thank you. I do appreciate this." I held the paper in the air.

It was all I could give him right now, and for some reason, I felt like he accepted it without judgment.

Maybe he wouldn't be such a bad friend after all. Who the hell would have thought?

TRYING TO KEEP IT TOGETHER

AVA

'D BEEN *OFF* all day. Elise had called and texted multiple times. She'd been doing it since last night actually, and I'd basically been ignoring her, trying to placate her with one-worded answers. She was eventually going to show up at my place if I kept putting her off, but I was too busy freaking out to talk.

When Tony hadn't been at the docks this morning, I had gotten nervous that he might have left. I was pretty certain he didn't fish because he had to even though I had no idea if that was true or not. But still, a part of me had assumed he didn't even need the money at all. Which only made me more unsettled. There was nothing and no one tying him here to Port Rufton, no matter how much I wished that weren't true.

Can't I be the reason he stays?

I had known that I'd make myself sick with worry if I didn't at least go check on his house. So, when I walked far enough up the road to where I could see his truck and noticed that nothing was packed in the back of it, my fear had settled slightly.

Tony was still here.

He might be avoiding me, but at least he hadn't bailed.

Not yet anyway.

I wasn't naive enough to believe that Tony would stay put if he grew too uncomfortable. The man could pick up and leave at any time. The notion didn't seem all that far-fetched. He liked to run. And he did it without warning.

My nerves reappeared and stayed that way all day long. No one had heard from him, and he hadn't been out on the water or gone out to check on his boat. Apparently, for a fisherman, that was a rarity.

The bell jingled over the door, and I glanced through the kitchen window to see my mother walking in. She was always so put together and beautiful, and today was no exception. Seeing her made me smile. Her eyes caught mine as she weaved through the crowd and made her way toward me in the back.

Wiping my hands on my apron, I moved away from the prep table right as she walked through the swinging doors.

"Hola, *mija*," she said in Spanish.

I watched as all the men in the kitchen practically melted at the sight of her. Everyone loved this woman.

"*Hola*," I said in response as we gave each other kisses on the cheek in greeting.

"Can we talk for a second?"

My mother never showed up at my job, wanting to chat, so I knew it must be important or time sensitive.

"In private?" I asked, and she nodded.

I waved my hand toward the back door, signaling that we should go upstairs to my apartment, and she immediately started walking.

"I'll be right back. The fish on the counter needs to go in the oven," I directed, and the guys instantly moved to take care of things. They seemed to be picking up my slack a lot these past few days. I felt almost guilty.

The door slammed closed behind me, and I followed my mother up the stairs and inside my place, where

Snickers greeted us both with meows. My mother bent down to scoop the cat in her arms, her long nails scratching behind my cat's ears. The purring was instantaneous.

"Is everything okay?" I asked the minute we were alone.

"I actually came to ask you that. I heard Liam and Tony got into a fistfight in the restaurant."

How had I forgotten that the town's rumor mill would eventually reach my mother? I hadn't even thought about it until now.

She continued telling me what she'd been told. "I heard the fight was over you. And they broke a bunch of stuff at the bar and got arrested. Although the bar looked okay when I just saw it."

"What?" I hoped my tone was as ridiculous as the story she was telling me.

"What?" she repeated, wondering what was so wrong about her information.

"You have bad intel."

"Bad what? What is intel?" My mother didn't always know or understand the meaning of certain English words.

"Your information is wrong. Liam did show up last night, but there was no physical fight."

Verbal, sure.

"Okay. Your Tony and Liam were both there though, right?" she pushed, trying to put the pieces in the right order.

My Tony.

"Yes. Apparently, the two of them know each other," I said before pressing my lips together.

"No." Her eyes grew wide with surprise. "How?"

"They used to work together."

"You're joking."

I blew out a breath, mixed with a slight laugh. "I wish. It was surreal."

"Well"—she put Snickers down and placed her hands on her hips—"what did Liam want? Why was he here?"

I shook my head. "I have no idea. I think he just wanted to ruffle my feathers."

My mother let out an annoyed huff. "You cannot be ruffled. Idiot." She walked the length of my living room. "He didn't say anything though? Really?"

"What are you getting at?" I asked because she was

acting weird. "What do you think he wanted?"

She stopped moving. "I wondered if he thought he might have claim to the restaurant."

I shook my head almost violently. "No. I made sure the divorce agreement stated that the restaurant was solely mine. He has no rights to it."

Blowing out a soft breath, she looked so relieved. "That's good."

"You were worried about that?"

"I was, but now, I'm not." She wiped her hands together, like she was brushing her cares away. "Tell me what happened with your Tony."

For almost two whole minutes, I hadn't even thought about the man.

"I feel wrong, talking about this, but you're my mother, so it doesn't count, right?"

"Mothers are exempt. They get free passes," she said, and it made me smile.

I gave her a very limited version of what had happened to him and his wife. Basically told her bits about the accident, but that was it. I left out the part where he had kissed me senseless and then told me to leave.

She whispered in Spanish to herself, mostly praying for Tony and his wife. After making the sign of the cross, she engulfed me in a hug. "I've seen the way you look at him, *mija*. Don't give up on him just yet. His heart is in pain."

I felt myself grow defensive even though it was completely uncalled for. "I know. I'm not giving up. I won't."

"He would never do what Liam did to you," she added, and I felt my eyes start to water.

"I know that."

I wasn't sure how I could be so certain, but I was. I felt it in my guts. Tony wasn't the kind of man to be unfaithful, no matter how trying times got.

A hard knock, followed by the turning of the knob, had us both staring at the front door. My pregnant best friend waltzed through it, an annoyed look on her face.

"You've been avoiding me." She started chastising me before noticing my mother. "Oh, hey, Ma."

"Hello, darling." My mother walked to Elise and gave her a hug and a kiss on the cheek. "How is my bambino?" She put her hand on Elise's stomach for a breath.

"*She's* doing good." Elise emphasized the gender, and my mother laughed.

"You're going to be so mad when *she's* a *he*," she teased, and Elise made a face. "I'll be on my way. You two have some catching up to do." My mother waggled her eyebrows at us before heading toward the door.

"See you later," I shouted at her retreating form.

"I'll drop off more goodies later," she said before disappearing, and I was grateful.

She hadn't been baking as often as usual, so I was lacking in the dessert department, which I did not like. If my mom was going to stop making sweets, I needed to figure out a new solution. My restaurant had to serve at least one dessert.

Elise cleared her throat, directing my attention to her. She stood the same way my mother had—hands on her hips, waiting for me to spill the details of last night. "I can't believe you've been ignoring me. I should punish you."

"How?" I wondered what she thought she could do to me that would count as punishment.

"I don't know." She waved me off like I was the

ridiculous one. "That's not the point. Tell me everything. I heard that Liam threatened to burn the restaurant to the ground and Tony said he'd kill him if he tried."

"I'm really starting to worry about this town." I shook my head.

The game of telephone was no joke. This was the perfect example of how twisted the truth became when too many people started telling it.

"So, it's not true then?" She sounded so disappointed.

"Not what you heard."

Elise walked to my couch and plopped down on it. "That's too bad. Greg and I would pay a lot of money to see Tony put Liam in his place. We talked about it all night."

My words must have taken a moment to hit her, or to actually set in.

She leaned forward and tilted her head at me. "Wait a second. Rewind. Not what I heard? What did happen then?"

I filled her in on what had really happened at the restaurant—how Tony and Liam had known each other previously and the things that they had said for everyone to overhear.

"You're leaving something out. I can see it all over your face." She pointed a finger at me and moved it in the air. "Plus, you're a terrible liar."

She wasn't wrong. I was a terrible liar, but I hadn't lied yet.

A crazed sound escaped Elise's lips. "You hooked up with him, didn't you?"

"How did you—" I stopped short before thinking that pregnancy brain must have turned my best friend into a magic little witch.

Her jaw went slack. "Tell me right now."

There was no point in denying it.

"He kissed me, told me he shouldn't have done that, and then asked me to leave."

"He what?" She shook her head, like it was all too much to comprehend at once. "Start from the beginning and tell me everything. It's the only way we'll figure out his stupid man brain."

So, I did. And when I finished my version of events, she stood up and placed her hand on her stomach and gave me a knowing look.

"He'll come around."

"That's it? That's your advice? He'll come around?" I wasn't sure why I was so annoyed, but her words felt less than a little helpful.

"He freaked out." She gave me a nonchalant shrug. "He'll get over it. He likes you. I give him two days, max."

"Two days, max, before what?"

"Before he shows up here and finishes what he started."

That made my heart leap inside my chest and a smile skirt across my lips.

"I really hope you're right."

"Don't worry; I am."

"Is this your pregnancy superpower? You just suddenly know things?" I asked because Elise hadn't had this ability before.

She was as clueless as I was, constantly struggling to read the signs and hints that guys threw our way.

"Yes," she said without hesitation.

I had no idea if she was messing with me or not, but her confidence made me believe her.

That, and the fact that I wanted what she'd said to be

true, so I held on to her words and prayed that Tony would come back.

TAKING WHAT HE GIVES ME
AVA

TWENTY-FOUR MORE HOURS had passed, and there was still no sign of Tony. He hadn't shown up at the dock again this morning, and all the hope I'd had yesterday was slowly blowing away with the breeze. The longer this avoidance went on, the less likely it felt like we could recover from it. Or that Tony would even want to.

Sometimes, it was easier to stay away.

I knew that feeling all too well. It was exactly what I had done when it came to my divorce—packed my things, moved back home, and never planned on talking to or seeing Liam ever again. We didn't have kids to fight over, so pretending like he didn't exist seemed like an achievable goal. Until I'd remembered that his parents still lived in Port Rufton and he'd most likely have to come back here at some point, but I'd figured he could still do that without seeing me. Apparently, that was too much to ask of him.

Shaking all thoughts of Liam from my head, I sorted my purchases from this morning, grabbing ice from the freezer and placing the fish on it. Once the fresh catch was back to being cooled, I went to work on creating our special herb and spice blend for the lobster rolls. We'd been selling more than usual this past week, and instead of wondering where the sudden influx of customers had come from, I did the math in my head and doubled the recipe.

A quick knock on the wood didn't stop me from mixing as I shouted, "It's open," at whoever was there.

A throat cleared.

It was raspy and caught on itself. My body shivered in response. Two rough steps against the groaning wood stairs alerted me that Tony was now inside the kitchen, watching me. I could *feel* him.

"Ava."

His gruff voice met my ears, and I wondered for a moment if he was okay. He didn't sound like it, and my heart sank.

I turned around slowly, my eyes catching his and

holding. His facial hair was longer and a bit unruly. His dark eyes bore circles that most might not have noticed, but I did. He looked so damn tired, and it took everything in me to not comfort him.

What is it about this man that makes me want to take care of him?

I stayed rooted in place, forcing myself not to move, even though my brain screamed at my legs to close the distance between us. He ran both hands down the length of his face, like he was working up the nerve to say whatever he had come here to say.

Oh no, what if he says he's leaving and he came here to tell me good-bye?

I wasn't sure I'd be able to take hearing it. I'd pretend I was fine, for his sake, but the disappointment would cover my heart like a cloak.

"I'm sorry," he finally said. "For the way I acted the other night." He swallowed hard and sucked in a long breath. "I'd like to make it up to you."

All the tension in my shoulders instantly faded away. "You would?"

Two more steps forward. "If you'll let me."

My heart started racing. He wasn't here to tell me he was leaving.

"What do you have in mind?" I asked, hoping to ease his discomfort because he sounded more than a little unnerved.

A half-smile appeared as he stepped even closer to my body, not stopping until we were toe to toe. I looked up, and my breath caught in my throat. Even in his unkempt state, he still looked downright delicious. It really wasn't fair.

His rough hand cupped my cheek, and I leaned into it, closing my eyes for only a second. It was just enough time. When I reopened them, his lips were moving closer, and I parted my mouth in response. I still wanted this man, and I had no plans to deny him.

He kissed me softly, but with purpose. It was an apology and an unspoken promise, all in one. Tony wanted to try, but he wasn't sure how.

When he pulled away, his hand still held me, his eyes staring into mine, asking if I was okay without saying the words. "What time will you be done tonight?"

"I'll probably be done by eleven. Ten at the earliest."

"And tomorrow, you close at four?" he asked, and I couldn't stop myself from grinning at the fact that he knew the restaurant's hours.

During tourist season, it seemed like a bad business decision to close the doors at all, but after my dad had passed, I'd soon realized I needed a day off. Or at least half a day. On Mondays, the restaurant closed at four. It wasn't much, but it was better than nothing. And even though I knew we could stay open until two a.m., I chose not to. It was just too much work for everyone, and there were other bars in town that people could patronize.

"Uh-huh."

"I'll see you later tonight, if that's okay."

"It is," I said even though I knew I'd be exhausted.

There was no way I was letting this opportunity pass me by. I could have told him no, or blown him off, or maybe made him work a little harder, but playing games wasn't really my style. And a part of me knew that Tony hadn't intentionally been trying to hurt me; he simply didn't know how to move on after what had happened with his wife.

He leaned down to give me another kiss, like we'd

done it a million times before. Like we'd get to do it a million times more. "I really am sorry."

"I know," I said as my heart filled with empathy for him and all that he'd gone through alone.

"Don't think I don't know that you're way too good for me," he said.

I grabbed his arm when he went to pull away. My fingers gripped the tendons and held on tight, stopping him from leaving that way.

"We don't know that for sure. Maybe you're too good for me," I offered with a laugh.

He shook his head. "We both know that's not true."

"You're right. I'm definitely the good one. You're the grumpy one."

That got an actual laugh out of him. "I'll see you tonight, Ava. And thank you."

I squinted my eyes in confusion. "For what?"

"Giving me a chance," he said before walking straight out the back door without looking back.

This version of Tony was a million times better than all the previous ones I'd met combined. I'd take it every day of the week, but I'd start with tonight.

TRYING TO MOVE FORWARD
TONY

'D SPENT THE last day and a half wallowing in a pit of despair. I'd been wrapped in memories of the past, trying to reconcile them in my head. I wanted to forgive myself for what had happened with Lydia that night, but I wasn't sure how to go about doing that.

I had been the one driving. I'd taken my eyes off the road. Those were the facts. Yes, it had been an accident, but I was the one who had caused it. The biggest issue was the belief that I could have changed the outcome if I'd only done one thing differently. Lydia didn't have to die. If only I hadn't been staring at her, I could have seen the ice and avoided it—or at least slowed down.

I honestly didn't know if that was true or not, but I'd been considering it for almost twenty-four hours straight. With one conversation about the accident, I'd been tossed back into a period of time where I was stuck, no longer moving forward, watching it all play out in my head on repeat.

If I couldn't sort through all the guilt, how was I ever supposed to move on?

I also hated the term *move on*, which was why I'd snapped when Ava said it the other night. It felt disrespectful. Like I was leaving Lydia behind and putting her away like she hadn't mattered.

And she had mattered ... so damn much. The woman had been my lifeline. Living without her at first had felt so impossible that I wasn't sure how I'd do it.

You haven't been living though, my thoughts reminded me.

They weren't wrong. What I'd been doing since she had died didn't really count as *living* by anyone's standards. Existing, yes. Living, no.

I'm not here anymore, baby. It's okay to let go. The voice spoke the words softly into my head, making me think I was losing my damn mind. I wasn't sure if Lydia's spirit was hanging out with me or if I was just imagining all the things that I needed to hear.

To be honest, I wasn't any closer to an answer when it hit me that I wanted to at least try. Before Ava, I hadn't wanted to do much of anything. She was a walking ray of sunshine, and a part of me couldn't bear to pretend like there wasn't something brewing between us. Not without a fight. Hell, not after that kiss.

Go tell her you're sorry, the voice instructed. Lydia or my subconscious. It really didn't matter which one it was because either was right.

Patting Barley's head, I told him to be a good boy and that I'd be right back.

I didn't even stop to check my reflection before going to Ava's restaurant, and it was a good thing too. If I had seen my face, I wouldn't have gone until I cleaned myself up, and honestly, I'd already wasted enough time.

TALKING TO AVA had gone better than I'd expected. If she had told me to get out and never come back, I would have listened and understood. But somewhere deep inside of me, I had known that she wouldn't. Her heart was as big as they came, and for some reason I couldn't explain, she was giving me a shot with it.

Barley wagged his tail and jumped up and down when I walked back through the door with a slight grin on my face. He sensed my change in demeanor and was properly supportive of it.

"Hey, boy. We're going to see Ava later," I said, rubbing his head.

Even though he had no idea what the heck I was saying, he seemed even more excited than I was about it.

"Well, she didn't say you could come, but I'm sure she wouldn't mind. Right? Ava loves you."

I walked in my bathroom and shook my head when I caught sight of my reflection. Ava should have screamed when she saw me, not looked at me with desire in her eyes, which was what she had done. The face staring back at me was at least still recognizable, not like it had been after I first lost Lydia. I had become a shadow of my former self, fading away right in front of everyone's eyes, and no one could have done a damn thing to stop it.

Turning on the water in the shower, I grabbed my razor and set it on the shelf. I wanted to look my best before going to her place later. There were a few other stops I needed to make as well before the shops closed for the night, so I needed to get a move on.

I GOT A text from Ava a little after ten, letting me know she was heading to her apartment and that I could swing by anytime if I was still up for it. She didn't trust me not to change my mind.

Holding Barley's leash with one hand and a bag in the other, we walked the short distance to her place from mine. Barley was pulling, and I was afraid I was going to drop the bag I was carrying, so I let his leash go. He ran straight toward the back door of Ava's restaurant and waited.

"This way, bud." I nodded toward the stairs that led to her place, and he started bounding up them, creating a ruckus.

The door swung open before I reached it, and Barley ran inside, his leash dragging behind him.

"Barley!" I shouted, but it was too late. He was gone.

Ava appeared. "I didn't realize you were both coming," she said before we heard a loud crash and the sound of a cat meowing loudly.

"Shit." I started hustling at the same time Ava shouted at her pet. "I forgot about your cat."

How could that have slipped my mind? I'd seen the cat before staring at me from its perch in the kitchen window. I chastised myself before getting inside and shutting the door behind me.

"What'd he break?" I asked because I knew it had to be Barley's fault. His giant tail was always knocking things off of tables.

"It's nothing," she said, but I saw the table lamp on the ground, thankfully not in pieces, like I'd feared.

Ava stood there, both hands on her hips as she watched Barley trying to reach her enormous cat, who was on top of the kitchen countertop, swatting her paws at him every time he jumped. Barley wanted to play, and the cat was not having any part of it.

"He's never seen a cat before," I said as I walked into the kitchen and put the bag down. "Want me to take him home?"

Ava's gaze swung in my direction. "No. They can work it out. Right? Dogs and cats can be friends, can't they?" She was clearly asking, and I had no idea, but I assumed it was possible.

"I've seen videos of it, so it definitely *can* happen."

Her cat started hissing, and Barley cocked his head to the side, fascinated by the sound but too dumb to understand that it meant the cat hated him.

"Snickers, don't you be mean." Ava reached for her fat cat, but it hustled out of her grasp just in time.

I laughed at the name. "Snickers. That's your cat's name? Boy or girl?"

"Yeah. Snickers is a girl. And don't you be mean either," she chastised me, and I quickly snapped my mouth shut.

"Your cat hates my dog," I informed, watching the way Snickers' tail was swishing in a such a quick motion that it looked like she might pounce and attack at any moment.

"Who could ever hate this face?" Ava asked before bending down to kiss Barley's nose.

He started licking her cheek, and she turned away, wiping the affection from her face.

Snickers let out a sound of disgust, and I had a new

mission in life—to win over Ava's cat and make it love me.

I reached inside the bag I'd brought, and the sound made Snickers turn her attention toward me. She pranced across the top of the counters, leaping over the sink with little to no effort, and I wondered how a cat that big could even get off the ground. She stopped at my side, silently asking me what I'd brought over and if anything was for her.

Meow.

"Think she'll let me pet her?" I asked.

Ava made a face and shrugged. "It only took me six months, but maybe? She loved my mother instantly."

"So, she might like me right away too?" I pressed, and Ava gave me a wicked grin. I liked seeing it on her face.

"I guess there's only one way to find out."

I moved my hand slowly toward the fattest cat I'd ever seen, a little terrified at what she might do to me. Cats always seemed unpredictable, so when she jumped up and pressed her head into my palm over and over before I scratched behind her ears, I felt like I'd won the damn lottery or something.

"Ha!" I said out loud, and Ava actually looked impressed.

Barley let out a whine, and Snickers hissed at him, clearly letting my dog know who was boss here.

Note: it wasn't any of us, not even the two humans in the room.

"Man, cats are kind of mean," I said.

"Tell me about it." She nodded in agreement before pointing toward the brown paper bag. "So, whatcha got in there?"

IS THIS A DATE?

AVA

I WATCHED AS Tony reached into the bag he had brought, not missing the fact that he had shaved and washed his hair. He looked downright edible. It was a bit of an upgrade from seeing him earlier, and I only meant that in the best way. He'd looked so sad before. Now, he actually looked like he was in better spirits.

Looking down at my clothes, I realized that I'd texted him before I even left the restaurant and hadn't had a chance to change before he was at my door.

"Don't," he said, breaking up my thoughts.

"Don't what?" I asked, wondering if he could read my mind.

"You look great." He gave me a grin as he pulled a bouquet of roses out of his paper bag of tricks.

Red roses. That meant that this was more than just a

friendly meeting. This was an actual date of sorts. *Maybe. Hopefully.*

Barley barked, his tail wagging, and Snickers continued to hiss at him in warning.

"I'm so sorry," Tony said for the millionth time. "I should run him home."

"No. He'll wear himself out eventually. And Snickers will pretend he doesn't exist at some point. It will be fine," I insisted, but I didn't really have a clue.

Maybe Snickers would maul Barley's face the second he went to sleep. Or maybe she'd use his fluffy body as a pillow for napping. Cats had a mind of their own. Half the time, it didn't even feel like I owned Snickers at all. It felt more like she had simply chosen to stay at my place and could decide to take her leave at any time.

"Do you have a vase?" Tony asked, and I tried to remember the last time anyone had given me flowers.

Liam *never* did once we were married. He had said it was a waste to spend good money on something that would die two days later, and in my young naivety, I'd acquiesced with his stupid statement even though I thought flowers were romantic and I didn't care how quickly they died.

"I do," I said before opening the cupboard underneath the sink and pulling one out. "These are beautiful. Thank you."

He took a step toward me and gave me a soft kiss. "You're beautiful."

My heart leaped into my throat as he turned back toward his oversize goody bag and pulled the next item from it.

"I knew it!" I practically shouted as I arranged the flowers into the vase.

I had smelled the seasoning and fresh baked bread before he even walked fully through my front door.

"Heard this was your favorite," he said before adding, "when you aren't eating seafood, that is."

Tony pulled out multiple pizza boxes with the familiar logo I'd always loved. I squealed when I saw them. Pizza from Lombardi's was my absolute go-to meal when I didn't want to cook and was tired of eating my own food. Mr. Lombardi wouldn't tell me his secret, but there was something special that he did to his crust. There were flavors in there that even I couldn't figure out. It was as infuriating as it was delicious.

"This is the best! Have you tried it?" I asked, wanting to smack myself right after. Lombardi's was the only pizza place in Port Rufton, so of course, Tony would have gotten it at some point since he had started living here.

"I have. It's really good."

"It's chef's kiss," I said, pressing my fingers to my lips and moving them away before what he had said a little earlier finally resonated in my brain. "Wait a second. You said you heard this was my favorite? Who told you?"

I wondered who Tony might have been talking to. If it were Elise, she wouldn't have been able to keep that information to herself. I highly doubted Tony was having deep conversations with my mother behind my back. Tapping my finger to my lips, I tried to figure out who it might have been.

"I should probably keep my sources to myself, but it was Rory," he said, waiting to gauge my reaction to the news.

"Wow." I felt surprise zip through me. "That's …" I searched for the right word. "Impressive? Shocking? Nice?"

Tony nodded. "It is all of those things. I was taken aback too, but he's a really good guy."

"I thought you hated him," I teased.

"I did. But now, I don't."

I shot him a look. "What changed?"

"I thought he wanted to date you. I couldn't like him then."

"He doesn't want to date me?" I asked with a curious tone, clearly trying to push Tony's buttons. But I liked seeing him a little worked up and admitting his feelings to me. Who knew if he'd ever do it again? "That's news to me," I said, pushing even more.

"Are you trying to get me riled up?" he asked.

I started laughing. "Maybe a little."

"Rory told me that I could have you. So, we're friends now."

I let out a choke, mixed with a laugh. "He said you could *have* me?" I emphasized the word *have*. "I didn't realize that Rory got to give permission on my personal life."

Tony turned around and leaned his back against the counter as his arms crossed over his chest. "Do you want us to be friends or not? I can go back to hating him if that's more fun for you."

"Definitely not. I want you two to get along," I said with an uncomfortable smile, but I meant it.

Tony and Rory actually liking each other instead of wanting to kill each other would make everyone's life easier. Or at least a little more pleasant. And I definitely didn't want them to be enemies, especially if I was the reason.

"Grab some plates," Tony directed.

I did as he'd asked before setting them on top of the table. He followed close behind. The three pizzas tempted me with their delicious scent as he placed them down and opened the top of each one.

"I got a bottle of wine too. Hope white is okay."

"You thought of everything. Roses. Food. Wine."

"I was trying to impress you," he said so quickly and honestly that it almost gave me pause. His dark eyes looked into mine with such intensity that our mutual desire lingered in the air between us. "Tell me it's working."

I nodded my head and placed a kiss on his scruffy cheek. "It's definitely working," I whispered into his ear before I passed him by to get to my seat.

I watched as he struggled to catch his breath, obsessed with the fact that I was the one who had made him that way.

WE ATE OUR pizza and drank the wine, and the liquor was definitely doing me a favor. There were things I knew Tony and I needed to talk about, and I was grateful for the way the wine made it seem possible by loosening me up and giving me a little liquid courage. Maybe that was why he'd brought it. He needed the help as well.

Barley had finally given up on Snickers and was currently passed out on my tiled floor, his tongue hanging out of his mouth. I honestly had no idea where my cat was. Probably plotting.

"So," I started to say, not wanting to put this on the back burner any longer, "can I ask you something that might be a little uncomfortable?" I swallowed my latest bite and quickly followed it with another sip of my drink.

"It is why I'm here, Ava. Look, I know I haven't been the easiest guy to get to know, but I told you things I haven't told anyone since it happened," he said, and I knew he meant the accident and losing his wife, Lydia.

I found it interesting that thinking of her didn't bring me jealousy or any other unhealthy emotions. There was an odd sense of peace that I got each time I imagined them together. For some reason, when I'd considered our situation before, I'd thought that I might feel competitive with her ghost, that I'd never be good enough or measure up, always living in her shadow. But it wasn't that way at all. I actually felt almost protective over her and her memory. The last thing I wanted to do was act like she never existed or that she hadn't been important in shaping Tony's life.

"I'm just going to go for it, okay?" I took another bite of pizza as I braced for his response, and he gave me a gentle nod as he waited. "Do you think you'll ever be able to forgive yourself?"

It was a loaded question. That kind of thing might be impossible for a man like Tony. Even though it wasn't his fault, how could you not blame yourself on some level? I knew that if the roles were reversed and it had been me driving, I would have struggled with plenty of self-blame.

"I don't know," he admitted, his voice filled with sincerity. "I'm honestly not sure that I have it in me to give."

I felt like I understood what he was saying even though I'd never been in his position before. "But do you want to?" I asked with trepidation although it was the more appropriate question of the two.

If Tony wanted to live the rest of his life in some kind of purgatory, no one was going to be able to save him. Not even me. But if he did want to figure out a way through this darkness and back into the light, I'd gladly hold his hand while we tried.

His dark eyes met mine. There was so much raging just beyond the surface. I wished I could read him with just one look, but I couldn't. Not yet anyway.

"I want to try. I don't know if it's possible. To truly forgive myself, I mean," he explained, and before I could add anything to the conversation, he continued, "I've kind of come to the conclusion that even if it's not, I still need to find a way to move forward."

I noticed that he said *forward* instead of *move on*, like I'd said the other night, triggering his anger.

"I'd like to help you." It was an offer and an ask, all in one.

"I can't do it without you."

"Tony," I breathed out, the emotions hanging like rain-filled clouds between us. "How do I help? What can I do?"

He shifted in his seat and swallowed, like he'd already given this particular question some thought well before I ever asked it. He cleared his throat. "First off, I need to know if that's okay with you."

I wasn't sure what he meant. "If what's okay?"

"That I might not be able to forgive myself. Do you think you can deal with that?"

It was a fair question. One I'd never even considered because I'd been so caught up in all of his emotions that I put my own on the back burner.

"As long as you talk to me and don't shut me out, I think it's something I can handle." I nodded, more for myself than for him. "I need communication. You have to talk to me."

I really hoped that was the truth. I'd never been with someone as complicated as Tony before, with a past that haunted him, but I also hadn't wanted any other man in quite this way before. It was written all over my face every time I even looked in his direction. The whole town knew it.

"I appreciate that. And I'll do my best to give you what you need," he said, his brow furrowing slightly. "I used to be good at talking. Lydia always said it was one of my best qualities, but I haven't been doing much of it lately, in case you haven't noticed."

I waved him off. "I'm sure it's like riding a bike."

"I'm sure it is."

"Okay then."

"Okay then," he repeated, giving me a soft grin. "Any other *uncomfortable* questions?"

Is he teasing me?

"I don't know. Those two seemed like the most important. I hadn't really thought beyond them."

I wasn't sure if I was being naive again, like I'd been with Liam, but it didn't feel that way in my heart. I couldn't possibly know what else I should be asking when I'd never dealt with anything like this before. It seemed like more of a *figure it out as we go* type of thing. This was new territory for both of us, but as long as we wanted to travel the terrain together, I was confident that we could make it through.

"Well, before you get too excited—because I'm clearly such a catch"—he finished off his glass of wine in one gulp—"I have to ask you for something."

My heart sank a little inside my chest even though it should have stayed in place because we'd made so much progress. "Ask."

"I've given this a lot of thought. And I think what I'll need the most—and honestly, I feel like I have no right to ask this of you—is patience. I'm going to need you to be patient with me, Ava, because it's been a while since I've done this, and I might not be any good at it anymore."

I looked around the room—at the roses he'd brought, sitting in a vase on the counter, and the delicious meal plated in front of us—and couldn't have disagreed more. "I think you're doing all right so far. And again, as long as you talk to me, we can get through anything."

Choosing each other every day and communication, I thought to myself. That would need to become our starting foundation.

"Choosing each other every day and communication."

His voice hit my ears, and I felt my eyes go wide.

"I said that out loud?"

He let out a laugh, and I swore it was like music to my ears. "You did, but I like it. So, with that being said, I'd really like to date you, if you'll have me."

I couldn't stop the smile from spreading across my face because I'd been dying to hear those words from his luscious lips for well over nine months now, but I'd been convinced it was most likely never going to happen.

"Is that a yes?" he asked, staring at my mouth.

"Of course it's a yes."

"I'm going to try my best for you, Ava—I promise you that. God knows you deserve so much better than me, but I can't give you up."

My heart melted with his admission. He sounded so sincere. The rest of my words disappeared, so I reached across the table, my hand covering his, hoping he would take my touch as the answer to any questions he might still have.

He pulled out of my grasp, but my disappointment only lasted a second before he slid his chair across the floor and pushed out of it, stalking toward where I sat, my eyes watching his every move. He looked like a man on a mission, and I was it—the mission in question.

As soon as he reached me, he pulled me to a stand, our bodies so close that we shared the same air with each breath we took.

"I'm going to kiss you now," he demanded, and I gave him what he wanted without complaint.

I'LL BE DESSERT
AVA

H IS MOUTH WAS on mine, so slow at first before I could literally feel him letting go and giving in. The kiss changed in the same moment he did. It turned possessive and filled with desire. His tongue was pressing against mine, his hand tight on the back of my neck, holding me firmly in place.

I gave in to him, silently letting him know that I'd go as far as he was willing to take us. And, yes, that included the bedroom. Giving myself over to Tony completely felt like the natural next step.

He kept kissing me, the groans escaping from some visceral place deep inside of him, and I grew nervous, thinking he might regret this.

Pulling away slowly, I cupped the side of his face and held him. "Do you want to stop?"

His eyes squeezed closed before he reopened them. A part of him seemed torn in half, between moving forward and letting go.

"I don't want to stop," he growled. "But if we keep going like this, I'm not going to be able to until I'm buried so deep inside you that I'm all you feel."

A devilish grin crossed my face. "I don't have a problem with that. Just so you know."

Tony swallowed. He genuinely looked conflicted.

"What is it? What's the matter?"

"I want to be inside you so badly that I can barely think about anything else," he admitted. "But Lydia was the last woman I was with."

I'd assumed that. "I figured as much."

Tony sucked in a ragged breath. Whatever he was struggling with was eating him up inside. "If we do this, will it erase her? She'll no longer be the last woman I was in. She won't be the last person I made love to. Does moving on mean letting go?"

"It doesn't have to," I quickly answered before wrapping my arms around his muscular body, holding on tight.

We stood there, hugging each other like our lives depended on it, while my brain tried to formulate the proper response to make this all okay.

"Making love to me means that we're starting something new. It doesn't mean that your love for Lydia has to end. And it won't. What you had with her will never die. It will never be replaced." I let him go enough so he could look at me. "You don't have to let Lydia go. Ever. All I ask is that you make a little room for me too."

"You're so fucking perfect," he said, and I felt his composure returning. We were going to make it through this, and we were going to be okay. "I want you, Ava. I've wanted you since I first saw you at the inn. You were glowing then, like the little ball of sunlight that you are, and those beams drew me in even though I didn't know a thing about you. I always knew though that I'd eventually run to you instead of run from you."

"I'm glad one of us knew because I sure didn't."

Tony reached for my hand and interlaced our fingers before asking me where my bedroom was. When Barley whined and started to follow us, Tony told him to stay put, and he listened. In order to keep Snickers out, I closed the door behind us. There was no telling what that cat might do.

"It's been a long time." He said the words like it was something to be ashamed of when it was the exact opposite.

Knowing that Tony could go without sex was kind of a turn-on. Too many men ran through women they didn't care about without even giving it a second thought, claiming they had *needs*.

"For me too," I said unabashedly.

I wasn't the kind of woman who slept around—not that there was anything wrong with that. My feelings wouldn't allow it; I got emotionally attached.

I opened up the drawer of my nightstand and pulled out a box of matches. Striking one, I lit the candle sitting on top and raced to the one waiting on the other side before the match went out. Lighting the other candle, I felt satisfied with the romantic glow they provided as I flipped off the light switch in my room and stood there, staring at Tony.

He moved toward my body slowly and with purpose. I had the feeling that everything we'd do would be that way.

Tonight would be about him, and I willingly let him take the lead. He was the one crossing emotional lines that couldn't be seen, only felt. The anxiety built up inside of me until I felt like I might burst apart.

"I'm on the pill, by the way," I blurted out, so he knew that we were protected. I was pretty certain he hadn't come over tonight with a pocket full of condoms.

"That's nice," he said, his voice gravelly and raw.

Tony reached for my clothes and started peeling them away one item at a time. My top fell to the floor, followed by my bra. When he tugged my pants down to my feet, I stepped out of them before he stopped and stared at my almost-naked frame. His breath hissed as he reached for my panties and pulled them down as well.

I stared at the bulge behind his jeans and watched as he pulled his sweatshirt off and added it to the pile of discarded garments. His shoulders and arms were chiseled from working on the water, his skin so tan that I wanted to run my fingers down every inch of it. He popped the button of his jeans and pulled the zipper down. My eyes almost bugged out of my head at his hardness there, just waiting to get out.

"Eyes are up here, sunshine," he joked, lifting my chin until we were face-to-face.

I held eye contact while he removed his briefs, not even daring to glance down. He closed the gap completely, his lips on mine, his tongue in my mouth.

I felt his hardness tap me on the thigh, and it took everything in me not to grab it and lead it in the proper direction. Tony lifted me up and moved me on top of the bed, gently placing me down like it took little effort. He followed right behind, straddling my body as our eyes held fast. Emotion filled the space between us, overflowing into the room. Our connection was intense. Palpable. And I felt it with every fiber of my being.

"I'm probably not going to last very long," he warned.

I gave him a soft kiss. "It doesn't matter."

Once he moved inside of me, there would be no going back.

I felt the tip of him at my entrance, and I spread my legs a little wider in response. Since it had been so long, I knew this was probably going to hurt a little. I held my breath as I waited for him to push in, but Tony moved excruciatingly slow.

My eyes met his as he leaned down.

"Kiss me," he demanded as he moved in and out of me, a little at a time, before finally going all the way in with one hard thrust.

"Ahhh," I breathed into his mouth as pleasure and pain rocked through my core.

He bit my bottom lip before running his tongue across it. Our tongues danced like they couldn't get enough. And his hands refused to stay still. One second, they were in my hair, and the next, they were running down the curves of my hips, fingertips splayed on my skin.

There would be no taking this back.

No more denying our connection or mutual desire.

This moment sealed the deal once and for all.

Tony never stopped kissing me. Not even after I came and tried to pull away to catch my breath. He didn't stop as he came inside of me either Only once he finally rolled to the side did he break the connection of our fused mouths, his hand still on my cheek, like he was afraid to let go of me completely.

I was fully satisfied in every way. Physically connecting with him had been unlike anything I'd ever experienced before. The air still felt charged with it.

"Do you feel that?" I wondered out loud before I could stop myself from saying it, and he smiled.

"I think we might be magic," he said, and I couldn't help but agree.

TURNING THE PAGE
TONY
THREE WEEKS LATER

B EING WITH AVA was far easier than I had given us credit for.

I'd been so worried, so wrapped up in my own head about everything, that moving forward seemed impossible at times. I'd gotten so used to convincing myself that I deserved nothing good in life that I actually started to believe it. Ava shot that thought down immediately. And when I had confessed to her one night that I thought I might self-sabotage anything good that I tried to have, she had refused to buy into that way of thinking as well.

Ava forced me to make good on my promise to always communicate with her, and honestly, it was my saving grace at times when I felt lost in the dark.

After our first night together, we'd barely spent any

nights apart. She was either at my place or I was at hers. Snickers still hated Barley, but Ava was convinced they'd become best friends at some point. I wasn't so sure, but I held out hope. Something I wouldn't have been able to do a couple of months ago.

I still struggled with feelings of guilt that would rear their ugly head out of nowhere, but whenever I did, Ava held on a little tighter. As much as I adored her, it was almost uncomfortable to feel *this happy*. I'd been shrouded in the shadows for so long, stuck in my pit of despair, that joy had become a foreign feeling to me.

But now, here I was, watching my girl shop for fresh fish at the docks, like I hadn't just been inside her earlier this morning. She was slowly becoming my world, if she hadn't been already.

Barley whined when he saw her, tugging at the leash I had him on. He used to be such a good listener, but these days, he sprinted off without warning whenever he caught sight of Ava, so I had to start tying him up.

Rory worked diligently across the way from me, adding fresh ice to his catch. I still needed to thank him properly for all of his advice, but I hadn't done it yet.

Wiping my hands on the hand towel I kept at my table, I headed in his direction.

"Morning," he said when he spotted me.

"I just wanted to tell you—" I started, and he put up a hand to stop me.

"It's all good, man. I'm glad you two are finally together." He gave me a smile before nodding his head in Ava's direction. "I've never seen her so happy before."

Warmth spread through my chest, but a part of me refused to believe it. "Even when she was with Liam? At the beginning? Or their wedding?"

Rory shook his head and made a face. "She was so young then. It's not the same. You can't even compare the two really."

His words struck a silent chord inside my chest. She had been young when she first started dating Liam.

"Thank you anyway, Rory. I needed a kick in the ass, and you gave it to me. You're a good friend." I almost stumbled over the words.

He reared his head back in surprise. "Friends, huh?"

"I think so."

"Then, you owe me, right?" he asked with a shit-eating

grin on his face.

I shot him a glare. "What do you want?"

"I need a wingman."

A loud laugh escaped from my lips. "You do not need a wingman. All the females in town love you."

It was true. The handful of single ladies left in Port Rufton all had their eyes on Rory, and any one of them would be ecstatic to land him.

"She's not a local."

"You want me to help you land a tourist?" I asked almost incredulously.

Tourists were usually fairly easy, from what I'd heard. There was something about a summer fling with no strings attached that appealed to people.

"I've seen her here for three summers now. She keeps coming back with her girlfriends. Just help me out, man."

Nodding my head as Ava headed our way, I agreed, "Okay. I have no fucking idea what a wingman does, but I'll help you."

"Yes!" Rory thrust his fist in the air as I made my way back to my table, where my girl was waiting for me.

"Hi, sweet boy," she said, petting Barley's head.

"Daddy's so mean, isn't he? Tying you up like this."

She looked at me and stuck her tongue out before I grabbed her by the waist and pulled her against me, kissing her for everyone to see.

"Stop calling me mean."

"Sorry, I meant, grumpy."

"I'm not grumpy anymore," I complained at the description, and she laughed.

"No, you're really not." She grinned before giving me a sweet kiss. "What did Rory want?"

"A wingman, apparently."

She shook her head slowly and turned in Rory's direction before shouting, "A wingman? Really? Since when do you need any help with girls?"

"Since you shut me down for that guy," Rory fired back, and Ava only rolled her eyes.

"Let me look at your goods, boyfriend." Ava started inspecting my catch.

It was honestly getting harder and harder to leave her in bed each morning, and lately, I'd been wondering how long I'd keep doing it. I enjoyed fishing, but selling to the restaurants and stores was supposed to have been temporary. Maybe I could start helping Ava at the restaurant instead. I made a mental note to bring the topic up later and feel her out.

"Let me look at your goods," I repeated, reaching for the button on her shorts, and she skirted away from my grasp.

This was how it was between us—comfortable and easy.

"Get a room," someone shouted, and I flipped them the bird without breaking eye contact.

"I've got to go. I'll see you later."

She stood on her tiptoes and planted a kiss on my cheek before I claimed her mouth possessively, giving the guys on the dock something to really shout about. I got to do things to that woman that they could only dream about.

But they'd better not be.

"HEY, BABE. I think it's time," Ava suggested the next evening as she changed out of her clothes and into some clean ones.

She'd actually left the restaurant early, which was a

rarity for my girl, but since Elise had just had her baby, she couldn't seem to stay away from visiting. Something about brand-new baby smells.

Anyway, I knew what she was referring to. We'd been having the conversation more and more frequently lately, multiple times a day even. It had been weighing so heavily on me that I'd even started talking about it in my sleep. Ava insisted that I take this step, claiming that it was one of the last ones I needed to take in order to truly heal. She was right, but I still dreaded it.

"I'm going to go visit the baby. I'll take Barley with me," she said before grabbing Barley's leash, and he sprinted to her side. "You can do this."

"I can do this," I breathed out, and she leaned down, pressing those fantastic lips to mine before walking out my front door.

I dialed the number, knowing that he would know it was me calling as soon as it started to ring. Unless he'd deleted my contact information or blocked me completely. I hadn't considered that scenario whenever I played this moment out in my head. It never ended well.

"Hello, sir," I said as soon as Lydia's dad answered.

There was a long pause, and I checked my cell phone twice to make sure the call hadn't ended or dropped. I wouldn't be surprised if he'd hung up on me, but he hadn't. He was just … waiting quietly on the other end of the line.

"I know it's been a long time, but I wanted to call you and tell you how sorry I am." I said the words, but I broke down as they came out. "I should have said it sooner."

I didn't know if I'd ever told him that I was sorry before this moment. I thought I had, but I couldn't be certain. At least, not a hundred percent. I'd been so caught up in my own grief that I couldn't remember what I'd done or said to anyone for months after the accident. My mind was a blank slate, where only fragments of information revealed themselves to me. None of them making any sense really. Half the time, I wasn't sure if something had really happened or if I'd made it up in my head.

My body tensed as I braced myself for the hatred, which I was convinced he still harbored toward me, to spill out across the line, but to my utter surprise, it wasn't there. I guessed we'd both moved into the acceptance phase of grief during our time apart.

"Oh, Tony," he breathed into the line, his voice shaking with emotion, which almost broke me apart completely. The only thing that he was mad about was the disappearing act I'd pulled without warning. He said that he'd lost a daughter and a son, all at once. But he also understood why I'd done it.

Then, Lydia's dad gave me the greatest gift of all—*he forgave me.*

Told me that the accident wasn't my fault and apologized for ever telling me otherwise. He said that grief turned some people into monsters and that he'd been no exception.

I cried.

He cried.

We ended the call, saying that we'd stay in touch. I wasn't sure I would even though I'd agreed to it. It seemed unfair of me to put him through more pain. His forgiving me was one thing, but him learning that I had moved on and was in love with someone new, getting to have a life while his daughter's had been cut short, was something else entirely.

It seemed like way too much to ask of a person ...

especially a father.

I held on to my cell phone, the tears still falling down my face as I replayed the conversation for a second time. The relief that coursed through me was unlike any other I'd ever felt. For the first time in a long time, I could truly breathe again. Deeply.

The weight I'd previously held firmly on my shoulders lifted. Not entirely, but a damn good chunk of it was gone, just like that. I'd gotten so used to carrying it that I'd forgotten what it felt like to live without it. I thought I might float away if I stepped outside. Surely, I had to be light as air now.

Sucking in a few measured breaths, I inhaled deep and slow, reveling in the way the air felt inside my lungs. I had to tell Ava. Jumping up from the couch, I shoved my phone in my pocket and headed off to find my woman and tell her the news.

And, oh yeah, that I loved her. Even though I suspected she already knew that part. Magic, remember?

NO MORE MR. GRUMPY
AVA
SIX MONTHS LATER

TONY WAS LIKE a whole new person. Okay, that wasn't necessarily fair because who he was at the core hadn't changed one iota. And I loved that about him. His tough exterior remained, but I knew the soft heart that beat inside.

The call with Lydia's father had been the biggest blessing, and I was so grateful that he'd found the strength to make it. It helped relieve Tony of any lingering guilt, self-hatred, and it opened his heart even wider.

Mr. Grumpy was officially a thing of the past.

Well, on most days anyway. He still brought him out sometimes when he wasn't getting his way or he hadn't gotten enough sleep. It would have been irritating if I didn't find it so endearing. Yeah, I had it bad for the guy, and I wasn't even sorry about it.

"Are you ready?" Tony walked up behind me and wrapped me in his arms.

"I can't believe we're going outside in this weather." I looked out of one of the windows and shook my head.

It was snowing. Half the businesses were closed today, including ours.

Tony worked with me at the restaurant now. He still fished sometimes and brought me everything he caught, but it was mostly for fun, and I couldn't count on him to do it daily. We came up with new recipes together, and he helped a little in the kitchen but mostly hung out at the bar. He was an incredible mixologist, and now, we not only had the best seafood in Port Rufton, but also the best fancy cocktails to go along with it.

"We're barely going outside. We're just going to the restaurant to grab the muffins and chowder to bring to the inn."

"The last time I did that, some guy fell in love with me from another room," I teased as I wrapped a scarf around my neck and pulled a beanie over my head.

We were bringing food to Elise and Greg, who refused

to take the baby out in this kind of cold. They were still navigating the new-parent thing and were apparently terrified of everything.

"Some guy, huh?"

"I didn't even know he was there. What if it happens again?"

Tony cocked his head. "What if some guy falls in love with you from the fireplace while you talk to Elise at the check-in counter?" he asked, giving me more details from the first time he saw me.

"Uh-huh. Yeah, it could happen."

He shook his head and gave me a half-smile. "Not likely."

"And why's that?" I stuck out my hip and waited for him to give me a good enough answer.

"Because you'll be there with me this time."

"So," I argued, clearly baiting him.

Before he could respond, the sound of Snickers's hissing made both of us split up and start looking for Barley. I'd spent the night at Tony's house, and I brought Snickers whenever I did. Sometimes, I caught the dog and cat sleeping together, but there were other times when I'd watch Snickers staring at Barley like he was a pest she needed to dispose of.

"They're in the bedroom. Snickers is under the bed, and Barley's trying to get to her." Tony's voice was muffled, and I knew he was on the floor as well.

When I walked in the room, I started laughing. Tony's legs were the only things showing, Barley's tail was wagging, and Snickers was on top of the bed, licking her paws.

"She's up here," I said, and Tony wiggled his way out from underneath.

"Seriously?" he asked before looking up and seeing Snickers watching him, her tail swishing back and forth. "Let's leave before they do something else."

Barley started hopping around the way he did when he knew we were leaving the house. He usually came with us, but it was way too cold outside. Not to mention the fact that he'd get wet and dirty and create more work for Elise at the inn, and then, basically, she'd kill me.

"Not this time, buddy. We'll be back soon."

He looked crestfallen as he sat, his puppy-dog eyes staring up at me.

"Be good," Tony instructed, and Barley whined before giving Snickers a look.

"Oh, buddy, we know it wasn't your fault," I said, giving him a reassuring pat behind the ears.

My cat lived to torment the dog, and we all knew it.

We walked outside, all bundled in our winter gear, before Tony turned around to make sure the door closed all the way. The last thing we needed was the pets getting outside and causing chaos.

"When are you going to move in with me?" Tony asked, and I shouldn't have been surprised.

He'd been asking me that for months. It wasn't that I didn't want to live with him or that I thought we were moving too fast. I just knew that I never wanted to give up my apartment above the restaurant. It had been mine when I had nothing else. I loved that place.

"We could rent it out during the busy months. Who wouldn't love to sleep above the best restaurant in town? And with that view ..." Tony kept talking until I finally caught on to what he was suggesting.

"Like Airbnb it?" I asked, and he made a noise that sounded like a yes.

"I already looked into it," he said before putting both his hands in the air. "Not to pressure you. Just for information's sake."

"But you don't even own your place. You're renting. Why would we move in there?" I complained as we walked down the hill carefully, making sure not to slip on the ice.

"I bought it," he said.

I stopped walking, his hand jerking my body before he realized that I wasn't moving anymore.

"You what?"

"The sale just went through yesterday. I bought the house, the little piece of land in the back, and the boat slip at the marina."

I started shaking my head in disbelief. This man—who, only a handful of months ago, couldn't even bear to have a personal conversation with other people—was now trying to convince me to move in with him and the house he'd just purchased.

It was crazy. This was crazy. *He* was crazy.

In the best way, of course.

"What would Lydia do?" I asked out loud, the question

lingering between us.

It had become one of our things. Whenever I wasn't entirely sure how I felt about a subject, I'd ask him what Lydia would do if she were in my shoes. It was my way of keeping her memory alive in a fun and lighthearted manner. At least, that was always my intention.

I'd promised Tony that him moving forward did not mean he had to forget. And I was doing my best to keep that promise.

"She'd have already packed her things and moved in without even telling me," he answered with a joyful laugh. "I would have been the last to know."

That made me laugh as well. "I really think I would have liked her."

"You would have loved her."

"We've both loved the same man," I said with a smile.

Talking about her was so rarely sad anymore. It had turned into something beautiful, and I was so appreciative of that.

"And he loves you." He lifted the bundle I was in as he searched for my mouth and kissed it hard. "I love you, Ava."

"I love you too."

"If you did, you'd move in with me."

"Fine!" I shouted into the snow-filled void.

We were alone on the street, steps from the restaurant, and my voice echoed in the air.

"You mean it?" He took me in his arms and started spinning us around.

"I mean, I should probably ask Snickers first."

"Don't you dare," he said before pressing another kiss to my freezing cold lips.

"We're going to get stuck like this," I mumbled against his mouth.

"We're not made of metal."

"But we are magic," I added, and a mischievous smirk covered his face.

"That we are, babe. That we are."

The End

Thank you so much for reading this grumpy-sunshine romance! I hope you enjoyed it as much as I did. I have loved writing these Fun for the Holidays books! They've brought me so much joy and made writing fun again!

There are twelve books now! One for each month of the year. I hope you'll read them all and then tell your friends to read them too.

Other Books by J. Sterling

Bitter Rivals—an enemies to lovers romance

Dear Heart, I Hate You

10 Years Later—A Second Chance Romance

In Dreams—a new adult college romance

Chance Encounters—a coming-of-age story

THE GAME SERIES

The Perfect Game—Book One

The Game Changer—Book Two

The Sweetest Game—Book Three

The Other Game (Dean Carter)—Book Four

THE PLAYBOY SERIAL

Avoiding the Playboy—Episode #1

Resisting the Playboy—Episode #2

Wanting the Playboy—Episode #3

THE CELEBRITY SERIES

Seeing Stars—Madison & Walker

Breaking Stars—Paige & Tatum

Losing Stars—Quinn & Ryson

THE FISHER BROTHERS SERIES
No Bad Days—a New Adult, Second Chance Romance
Guy Hater—an Emotional Love story
Adios Pantalones—a Single Mom Romance
Happy Ending

THE BOYS OF BASEBALL
(THE NEXT GENERATION OF FULLTON STATE BASEBALL
PLAYERS)
The Ninth Inning—Cole Anders
Behind the Plate—Chance Carter
Safe at First—Mac Davies

FUN FOR THE HOLIDAYS
(A COLLECTION OF STAND-ALONE NOVELS WITH HOLIDAY-
BASED THEMES)
Kissing my Co-worker
Dumped for Valentine's
My Week with the Prince
Fools in Love
Spring's Second Chance
Don't Marry Him
Summer Lovin'
Flirting with Sunshine
Falling for the Boss
Tricked by my Ex
The Thanksgiving Hookup
Christmas with Saint

About the Author

Jenn Sterling is a Southern California native who loves writing stories from the heart. Every story she tells has pieces of her truth in it as well as her life experience. She has her bachelor's degree in radio/TV/film and has worked in the entertainment industry the majority of her life.

Jenn loves hearing from her readers and can be found online at:

Blog & Website:

www.j-sterling.com

Twitter:

www.twitter.com/AuthorJSterling

Facebook:

www.facebook.com/AuthorJSterling

Instagram:

@ AuthorJSterling

If you enjoyed this book, please consider writing a spoiler-free review on the site from which you purchased it. And thank you so much for helping me spread the word about my books and for allowing me to continue telling the stories I love to tell. I appreciate you so much. :)

Thank you for purchasing this book.

Sign up for my newsletter to get emails about new releases, upcoming releases, and special price promotions:

NEWSLETTER

Come join my private reader group on Facebook for giveaways:

PRIVATE READER GROUP

facebook.com/groups/ThePerfectGameChangerGroup

Made in United States
Troutdale, OR
10/14/2023

13694959R00105